G

M000073227

ANOTHER SUMMER IN THE OLD TOWN

Copyright 2009 by Randy Cribbs

Library of Congress Control Number: 2008935527

ISBN: 9780972579674

Published by OCRS, Inc.

Printed in the United States of America

To obtain books go to www.somestillserve.com

or write OCRS, Inc.

P.O. Box 551527

Jacksonville, Florida 32255-1627

Also by Randy Cribbs:

One Summer in the Old Town

Ancient City Treasures

The Vessel

Tales from the Oldest City

Were You There? Vietnam Notes

Illumination Rounds [coauthor]

GHOSTS

ANOTHER SUMMER IN THE OLD TOWN

To: the Kishner Kids

Happy haunting!

Randy Crib
2009

Randy Cribbs

OCRS, Inc., Jacksonville, Florida

Dedicated to my best fan,

my wife Sherry

PROLOGUE

July 3, 1900, St. Augustine, Florida

John sat up, totally alert, tensed, listening. He could hear the quiet breathing of his two cousins on the bed a few feet away. The snores of his uncle in the next room verified the sheriff also was asleep.

John wasn't sure what time it was, but knew it was very late.

From across the hallway he heard the cough of a prisoner in the cellblock. Carefully feeling around the floor under his small bunk, John located his clothes and, without a sound, slipped on his trousers.

Someone coughed. John stopped and held his breath, alert to any other sounds. If his uncle caught him sneaking out, there would be the devil to pay.

He pulled on his shabby leather shoes and stood up, pausing to listen again. Ever so cautiously he tiptoed to the door, opened it and took one last look back. Everything seemed normal, so he eased through the doorway, closing the latch softly behind him.

Now standing in the damp cellblock hall, he could hear the sleep sounds of prisoners. Moving with great care, John made his way down the iron steps knowing that any noise on cold iron would be amplified in the quiet darkness.

At the bottom of the stairs he turned right and headed to his uncle's office on the first floor. He entered quietly and moved through the office to the next room, which served as the family parlor. Moonlight seeped through the rear windows and verified his friend Daniel's forecast of a bright, clear night. Pausing at the window, John listened again and could still hear the faint snoring from his uncle's bedroom directly overhead.

Mindful of the creaky hinges he slowly opened the window. John's exit was a slip from the windowsill and a short fall to the ground. Scrambling quickly to his feet, he listened for any movements from the guards.

How did I ever let Daniel talk me into this? he wondered.

He cautiously made his way around to the rear of the jail. The stout board structure of the gallows silhouetted starkly against the moonlit sky and a million stars. He shuddered and looked away.

Feeling more confident about his escape, he walked in a crouch toward the rear gate.

"I see you, little boy," a voice from the sky said.

"Mary, be quiet!" John hissed softly.

"You're up to no good. Sheriff's gone git you," Mary said in her whiny, singsong voice, accompanied by her eerie giggle.

"Be quiet before you wake everybody," John urged again, as loud as he could whisper.

"Maybe Mary just tell dat ol' sheriff you came out here." Her weird cackle followed.

"If you stay quiet and don't tell, I'll get you extra grits in the morning."

"And hoecakes?" she whispered.

"Hoecakes too. Now be quiet!"

Mary turned from the cell window, mumbling to herself.

Finally on the street, he headed for the bay front, glancing back every few seconds to ensure no

3

one was in pursuit. As the jail disappeared behind him, he picked up his pace, knowing Daniel was probably already waiting for him.

With the jail no longer in sight, John felt a growing sense of excitement and broke into a run. Feeling more confident about the adventure ahead, he was anxious to get to the rendezvous point.

When the old fort came into view he stopped to catch his breath and took another quick look behind him. But the Nation's Oldest City slept. No movement and only an occasional dog barking disturbed the silence. John rounded the fortress and headed toward the seawall. He heard lapping water and saw Daniel on the shore holding the rope to the small boat. The inlet sparkled and danced under the soft glow of light from a moon unfettered by clouds.

"Where you been? I been here forever," Daniel said to John, who now stumbled down the bank and fell in a heap on the sand. "Come on, come on," Daniel urged, "it's perfect."

"Daniel, are you sure about this? We're gonna be in big trouble if we get caught, and what if something happens?"

"Nothing's gonna happen. Who's the strongest swimmer in town?"

"You are," John replied to his closest friend.

"That's right, and look at that water, how calm it is. It's gonna be great! And the moon's so bright, it's like daylight. Come on."

"I don't know why you can't wait till tomorrow. Your father said he'd take you out then."

Losing patience, Daniel looked at John. "Because tomorrow I'm gonna show him I can sail this boat, but I need to practice tonight." He pointed to the small sixteen-foot boat rocking gently on the surface. "He's gonna be proud of me."

"Well, I don't know," John said.

"John, don't I always take care of you? Nothing's gonna happen. It'll be fun." Daniel turned to the boat. "Now come on, help me shove out."

John moved to the boat and helped Daniel push the small craft to deeper water. As the cool water came up around his legs, John felt his anxiety ease and his sense of adventure take over. Besides, he trusted his friend—always had.

They turned the boat toward the open bay, gave one last shove and scrambled in. Daniel grabbed the rope connected to the sail mast and instructed John to take the rudder. The heavy canvas unfolded up the short pole. Daniel secured the rope and surveyed the sail hanging lifeless from the gently swaying mast.

"Head us straight out while I try to find the wind," Daniel said.

The boat gradually picked up speed when a soft breeze began to fill the sail. John breathed in fresh salt air as he watched his friend jockey the boom. Maybe Daniel had a good idea after all, he thought.

Daniel looked back and laughed. "See, I told you this would be fun. Look how calm it is."

They maneuvered the boat around the end of the fort and headed toward the wider part of the bay. Suddenly the boat swerved and tilted violently to the left.

"What are you doin'? What's wrong?" John yelled in a frightened voice.

"Nothing. Boom just slipped. Don't worry," Daniel said while grappling with the rope.

The boat steadied, picked up speed and headed into the open night.

"OK. This is a good course," Daniel said, using his best captain's impression. "Come take the boom for a while."

"No, I don't know how."

"There's nothing to it. Come on, I'll show you."

John reluctantly took the boom and soon got the hang of it.

"Hey, you're right. This ain't so bad," he said to Daniel with a huge smile.

"See, I told you so," Daniel said, and gave a satisfied laugh.

John liked the gentle jerk of the boom rope in his hand as the sail rippled and flirted with a soft breeze.

"We better turn around and head back," Daniel suggested several minutes later. "I wanna try a turn and we don't wanna push our luck. Let me take the boom."

John stepped awkwardly to the back while Daniel started a wide turn to head back toward the fort.

"Daniel, Daniel, what's that?" John yelled when they were halfway through the turn.

"What?" Daniel said, turning to John. When he saw his friend's expression, he jerked his head back toward the front of the boat.

Directly ahead, a great three-masted vessel with a cloud of canvas aloft was bearing down on them and the boat.

"Holy cow, he's comin' right at us!" Daniel yelled. He swung the boom as hard as he could. "Turn the rudder hard as you can," Daniel yelled. "He's gonna hit us!"

But John's hand was frozen to the rudder; he could only stare in terror at the quickly approaching ship.

"Jump!" Daniel yelled.

John gave a quick cry, shut his eyes and clasped his hands over his face. An instant later the shattering roar of the small boat being crushed under the huge ship deafened the two boys.

It was over in an instant and a stunned moment later, Daniel popped to the surface, gasping for air.

"John," he yelled frantically to the silent night. He could see the rear of the tall ship fading away.

"John, John!" Daniel cried out, near panic.

He saw movement off to his right. Daniel was oblivious to the debris hitting his body as he swam toward his floundering friend. John went under just as Daniel reached him. Frantically, he dove and grabbed his shirt.

"John," he yelled again as they broke the surface.

John moaned but did not reply. With John's shirt firmly in his grasp, Daniel looked around trying to get his bearings. He could barely see the outline of the fort. With John in tow, he headed that way.

Soon, his strength fading, Daniel had to stop. Desperately he tried to tread water and hold John's head above the lapping waves.

In a barely audible voice, John said, "I can't make it. You go." Blood trickled over his face.

"You can make it! I'm not leaving you! I'll never leave you. You're my friend," Daniel said, resuming his effort to tow John toward shore.

But it was too much.

Daniel's strength failed. His last thoughts were of his parents and how angry and hurt they would be.

CHAPTER 1

St. Augustine, modern day.

"Lady, for the last time, there is no fire and there are no people in there!"

The fire chief turned from the Old Jail and signaled his fire crew to uncouple and roll up the hoses. The flashing red lights of the trucks moved away.

The chubby woman wearing a St. Augustine tank top and flip-flops turned to a city policeman standing by. "I tell you, we saw a fire flickering in that room and at least two people moving around! Tell him, George," she said, turning to her husband for support.

"She's right, Officer. We both saw it," the beleaguered man said, shrugging.

The cop said, "I know. I know, folks. But the chief cleared the building and there's nothing there. The Old Jail is just a museum now. There's no one there at night."

"Well, of course we know it's a museum. We went through it yesterday. The fire we saw seemed to be where the fireplace is in the old parlor. That's why we called. We knew no one should be in there, and we saw at least two people moving around—wavy-like, maybe from the smoke."

"Yes ma'am. Well, there's no signs of a fire and like I said, there's no one in there. I have your statement and we're going to keep our eyes on the place for a while. We really appreciate your concern." He touched the brim of his hat with a finger and added, "Now, you folks enjoy the Old Town and thanks again."

As the couple walked away, the woman mumbling to her husband, the police officer took a last look at the quiet building and headed for his patrol car.

11

CHAPTER 2

Matt stepped off the front porch and went down the old coquina brick steps two at a time. The late afternoon Florida sun caused him to squint. He reached into the motorcycle helmet dangling from his hand and pulled out his sunglasses. After adjusting the shades just so on his nose, he surveyed the empty tree-lined street of the historic downtown St. Augustine neighborhood.

He walked across the front yard and turned toward the driveway where his covered cycle awaited his commands. Placing the helmet on the ground, he carefully removed the cover and stowed it on the side door stoop.

With a soft, folded cloth produced from his rear pocket, he wiped the already clean, shiny tank and fenders of the motorcycle. He then retrieved the helmet and straddled the worn leather seat, and with a slow, deliberate movement, raised his helmet and slipped it on his head. Purposefully, he threaded the helmet restraining strap and gave it a melodramatic tug.

Next, left hand inserted into the thin leather glove. A tug, followed by the slow finger flex. Repeat right hand.

He felt a rush as he reached for the ignition of the old motorcycle, anticipating the roar.

He had left his sixteen-year-old body and was about to become a great adventurer, riding his rumbling steel Beast. He caressed the ignition key.

"Matt."

Startled from his fantasy, he jerked his head around. He mumbled, "Oh. Hi, Jenny."

Jenny had a mischievous smile on her pretty face. "That was quite a show," she teased.

"Just saddling up," he said, using the motorcycle language he had gone to great extremes to learn. "Anyway, at least I'm riding a real cycle, and not a toy." He nodded toward her pink moped parked in the driveway next door.

Striking a thoughtful pose, she circled the '50s-era Indian motorcycle with its bullet-nosed sidecar. "If you say so," she finally said with the laugh that always caused Matt to blush. "Anyway, I just wanted to see if Sean is still coming in tomorrow."

"Oh, yeah. Mrs. Kirk says he'll be here in the afternoon," he replied, referring to Sean's grandmother, who lived across the street. "We talked on the phone last night. Sean says he's looking forward to his fourth summer in the Old Town. Can't wait to get out of New York for a while."

"When does he start working at the Old Drugstore?" she asked, referring to the summer job Matt's dad had arranged for his son's friend.

"I'm gonna take him over to meet Lynn as soon as he gets here, and he starts the next day. I'm on my way to the Old Jail for my first official day now." He reached for Jenny's wrist to check her watch and felt a slight tingle. "Well, guess I better go," he mumbled, not wanting to remove his hand. "Say, Jenny, I was wondering if, ah, well, you know the July Fourth thing. I, ah, well, I was just thinking." He paused, his throat seeming to constrict.

Jenny glanced at his hand lingering on her wrist, and looked back at the helmeted teenager curiously.

"Well, anyway ..."

"Jenny." He was cut off by the girl's mother. "Hurry, honey, we're late."

"Oh jeez," Jenny said, a hint of disappointment spreading across her pretty face.

"It's OK, I gotta get going. I'm late too." He reluctantly released her wrist.

She smiled and covered her ears as the old bike roared to life.

Matt guided The Beast down his street, turned left onto San Marco and headed toward the Old Jail and Museum, wishing it was more than a four-minute ride.

He was still in the "getting used to it" phase with the motorcycle. His grandfather, Honeyman, had Matt's promise to stay in town, short trips only, till he was more experienced—a major condition for the gift that had been stored in Honeyman's garage on the St. Johns River for almost forty years.

Tourists strolling both sides of the brick street turned to see him pass, causing him to straighten his back, conscious of preserving the *Easy Rider* image.

He turned into the jail parking lot, almost empty at 4:30 P.M., and parked. He glanced around to ensure no one had seen his less than smooth stop.

"You're almost late."

"Oh, hi Mr. Usina," he said to the man standing in the tour trolley station.

"Come on, let's get started."

A man of few words, thought Matt.

"Now, you've taken the jail tour a couple of times and you've had your duties explained to you. You got any questions?"

"No sir. I go see Heidi in the gift shop and help her until the last tour, then I go the tour route through the jail and pick up stuff and make sure everything is in order for the next day."

"And?"

"Oh yeah, I pay particular attention to the sheriff's quarters and make sure everything is arranged right in case people have moved stuff around while they were touring."

"You got the diagram that shows how items are arranged?"

"Yes sir."

"OK. Go see Heidi."

Matt turned toward the gift shop.

"Oh, Matt."

"Sir?"

"Don't get locked in there now. It is haunted, you know."

"Oh, yes sir. No way." Matt laughed.

Mr. Usina didn't laugh.

Matt scurried away and found Heidi stacking boxes in the gift shop.

"I see Mr. Usina was playing with you. It's not really haunted, you know—at least, I don't think it is." She raised up from the box she had just emptied. "But there are those noises every now and then. ... Why don't you take these boxes out to the trash? By then the last tour will be finished, and you can make your rounds," she said with a chuckle.

"You bet. No problem." Matt often found himself wishing people wouldn't treat him like a kid. Besides, most sixteen-year-olds didn't drive classic Indian motorcycles.

After the last box was crushed and trashed, he turned to his main duties. The sun disappeared behind an empty parking lot.

Matt picked up trash by the old gallows and found everything in order in the solitary confinement cell and the kitchen. He approached the door to the downstairs part of the sheriff's quarters, reminding himself to do a good job arranging the museum artifacts, suspecting Mr. Usina would check.

Matt stood in the doorway and surveyed the sheriff's office, the first room to check before moving to the rear parlor.

He stepped into the room but stopped when warm air rushed over his face. He looked through the office to the rear window of the adjoining parlor.

Closed.

He glanced at the ceiling. No fan.

Matt scoffed at his silliness and stepped forward, only to hit some object which sent him tumbling to the floor.

As he scrambled up to confront whoever tripped him, he heard a low, twangy giggle—a girl, maybe.

Matt looked for signs of another person, but he was alone.

What had he tripped over? Checking the immediate floor area, he found nothing but the floor and open space.

"Scared little boy."

"What …" Matt said aloud. "Who's there?" he demanded of the empty room.

He retreated to the hallway to regroup, staring back into the room.

A few seconds passed and nothing happened. Finally, attributing the episode to his first day alone in this old, strange place and imagination gone wild, or more likely a joke on the new kid, he stepped into the office again, and this time proceeded all the way through to the parlor.

All was well.

Nevertheless, he completed his tasks in the two rooms and made a beeline to the stairs for his upstairs checks.

CHAPTER 3

Mrs. Kirk probed the large cake with a toothpick and grunted with satisfaction. As she closed the oven door she heard a racket outside and moved to the window. Peeking out, she saw Matt arriving home from his dental appointment on that silly contraption Honeyman had given him.

Moving as fast as her legs would allow, she opened the door and called out to the young boy, who was still wrestling with his helmet strap.

"Oh, hi Mrs. Kirk," replied Matt to her greeting. "I guess they haven't got here yet, huh."

"Not yet," she said. "They should be here any minute. Come on over and sit on the porch with me."

"I can't wait to see Sean again," he said while settling into a rocking chair next to his neighbor. "And I think he'll like working at the Old Drugstore."

"Oh, I know he will. We're so grateful to your dad for getting him that job. How about you? You started at that Old Jail yet?"

"Yes ma'am, I had my first day there yesterday, and I like it OK, but it's kinda weird."

"What do you mean, kinda weird?"

Matt hesitated while recalling the strange experience he had in the sheriff's office. "Nothing, really," he replied. "You know, it's just a really old place."

"Yes, it is old. Probably a lot of stories in there." She gave Matt a sideways glance.

They rocked quietly.

Mrs. Kirk stopped rocking and turned to face Matt. "Some say that place is haunted. Course, they say everything is haunted in the Old Town." She watched the boy fidget in the rocker. "What do you think?" she asked.

He mumbled, "No, I, ah, well, no. I mean there aren't really ghosts. I didn't see any ghosts."

She resumed a slow rocking. "Well, just remember, if you do see any—" She stopped in mid-sentence when Matt's dad and Sean pulled into the driveway.

Unable to contain his excitement, Matt leapt from the rocker and in two bounds was standing by the Jeep.

"Sean!" he yelled. "'Bout time."

Sean was out of the vehicle as soon as it stopped.

"You got taller," Matt said. He playfully punched his friend on the shoulder.

"You too, dude, but you're still not quite as pretty as me," Sean replied, laughing.

"Everybody's taller and pretty," Matt's dad said, joining in the playfulness. "Now, let's get these bags in the house."

Mrs. Kirk grabbed Sean in a bear hug while he struggled onto the porch with bags in each hand.

"Grandma, you're gonna knock me down the steps," Sean said, laughing.

"Don't worry, I'll catch you."

"Jenny!" Sean exclaimed as he appraised the young girl standing on the lower step. "You've, ah ... changed."

"Is that one of those New York boy left-handed compliments?" she teased.

"No. No. Oh, you know what I mean," Sean replied, caught off guard.

"In that case, I forgive you." She gave him a quick peck on his cheek.

Matt observed the exchange with a small twinge of jealously, but it quickly passed because he knew Sean was aware that Matt was particularly fond of Jenny. Sean had tried to convince him last year that Jenny felt likewise, but Matt had little confidence when it came to the fairer sex. His awkwardness in showing affection for the girl was frustrating. He just couldn't think sometimes when he was with her. Jenny, on the other hand, with her extroverted personality and witty sense of humor, seemed to have loads of fun with that situation.

"Well, everybody come on in the house for cake," Mrs. Kirk said, rescuing the teenagers from the current dilemma. She exchanged smiles with Matt's dad.

After the better part of Mrs. Kirk's famous pineapple upside-down cake had disappeared and the lively catch-up conversation had slowed, Matt's dad stood up.

"That was great, Mrs. Kirk. You're still the best cake maker in the Old Town," he said, touching her fondly on the shoulder.

"Oh, pshaw. You go on." The old lady beamed. "Thank you so much for picking up Sean," she added.

"You know it's always a pleasure. Come on, Matt, let these folks visit a while. You're supposed to drive Sean over to the drugstore to meet Lynn, aren't you?"

"You got your license too, huh," Sean said in a casual teenager manner, suggesting everyone had a license.

"Oh yeah. Had it several weeks," Matt said, with a little pride in his voice. "You too, huh?"

"Yeah, soon as I turned sixteen, but I don't get to drive much. My dad says New York City ain't the place to practice driving." He eyed Matt. "Don't tell me you got a car?"

"Well, not exactly."

"I'll say, not exactly," Jenny said.

Matt pushed her playfully, as his dad chuckled and said, "You'll see soon enough, Sean."

Matt followed his dad and Jenny through the doorway. "Come on over in an hour or so. I'll drop you at the drugstore on my way to the jail. When you're done, you can walk up to the jail and I'll give you the tour. Pretty neat. You remember how to get there?"

"Oh yeah. No problem. See you in an hour."

CHAPTER 4

Matt shoved a helmet into Sean's hand when he answered his knock at the door.

Sean glanced at Jenny's pink moped parked in the adjacent driveway. "If you think I'm getting on the back of that motorized flamingo, you got another think coming."

"No way! That's Jenny's. Follow me, man."

They stepped off the porch and Matt led the way around the Jeep to where The Beast sat.

"What is that!" Sean exclaimed, examining the old bike.

"Hey, watch your tone. *That* is a classic 1954 Indian motorcycle. Honeyman gave it to me when I got my license."

Matt gazed with adoring eyes at the bike. "I call it The Beast. Very powerful, you know."

"I'd say that's a good nickname." Sean walked around the bike. "And the box?"

"It's not a box, dummy. It's a sidecar. That's where you go. Put your helmet on."

Sean looked from Matt to the sidecar and then back to Matt. "You want me, the New York kid, to get into that?"

"Hey, it's only a mile. Scared you can't handle it?" Matt challenged.

"I'm from the big town, remember." He shook his head from side to side. "At least I don't have to put my arms around you." He began wrestling his way into the cramped passenger compartment.

"All comfy?" Matt asked with a big grin.

"Don't push your luck, dude." He slapped his helmet and pumped his fist up and down. "Let's do it, Evel Knievel."

The engine roared to life, made a coughing sound and died.

"Well, that's a good start," Sean said, unable to resist the jab.

"It's just a little cold-natured. Sometimes you have to cuddle it." Matt rubbed the gas tank as he would his pet. "Come on, Beast," he said, turning the ignition key again.

The engine caught and purred in a low rumble.

"See, it's got personality. You gotta know how to handle it."

"Yeah, yeah, yeah. Let's go before I lose all feeling in my legs."

Though it seemed like more to Sean, they arrived at the Old Drugstore five minutes later. The store owner was on the rear deck watering her plants.

"Oh great, there's Lynn. I'm running late. Hey Lynn," Matt yelled.

She put down her watering pitcher. "Hi Matt. Is that my summer help you have stored in your luggage compartment?"

"It's a sidecar, Lynn, and I'm late. This is Sean."

Matt watched Sean struggle out of the sidecar. Nodding his head toward the Tolomato Cemetery next to the drugstore parking lot, Matt asked, "Hey Sean, remember that place?"

"Do I ever!" Sean said as they both laughed.

"OK. I'll see you at the jail when you're done here," Matt said.

Sean finally freed himself from The Beast. "Yeah. I'll critique you as a jail tour guide, so be sure to rehearse before I get there."

Matt shook his head and rode off to his job.

"Come on in, Sean," Lynn said. "I'll tell you about the drugstore and your job."

"Yes, ma'am."

"Oh my goodness, manners! How delightful to see the genteel nature of the South rubbing off." She laughed pleasantly. "Come on, I'll show you around."

After almost an hour of meeting people, touring the store museum and having various duties explained to him, Sean's head was spinning.

"Tell you what, since it sounded like you're meeting Matt at the jail, why don't you haul all those boxes over to the Dumpster, and then take off?" Lynn suggested, noting his worried look. "You're gonna be fine. You'll catch on in no time." She pointed toward the cemetery corner. "See the bin there by the graveyard fence?"

"Yes ma'am."

"Good boy. See you tomorrow." She turned to greet a group of tourists.

CHAPTER 5

Sean threw the last box into the bin and turned to leave. He smiled as he recalled Matt's question about the cemetery. Walking up to the fence, he started laughing while visualizing the trick they had played on the bully, Riley, three summers ago. He had told his friends the story many times.

Sean picked up a pebble and threw it, like he had done that night three years ago.

Clink. ... Clink. ... Clink.

Matt jerked awake.

Clink.

He jumped from bed and ran to the window, where he saw Sean was preparing to toss another small rock to get his attention. Matt raised the window and peered out. The night air hit him, hot and sticky.

"Come on, man, we'll be late," Sean whispered. "Get Walter, Jenny has the cage."

Matt handed Walter out to Jenny. Without protest, the cat went into the cage and looked around.

"OK, he's fine. Come on," she whispered. "Did you remember to put the reflectors up?"

"Yes. Let's go."

It was almost midnight, and dark when they arrived at the graveyard. No one was around, so they went ahead and climbed the short chainlink gate.

They crept forward cautiously, the dry leaves crunching under their feet. The anxious teens were unable to hide their quickened breathing.

"E-e-e-e-e-e."

"What was that?" Jenny grabbed Matt's arm in a viselike grip.

A large bird abandoned its treetop at the intrusion.

"It's a bird," Matt whispered. "Jeez, let go," he added, trying to free his arm from Jenny's grip.

"Sorry."

They started forward again, more closely bunched.

"OK. Remember the plan," Jenny said, making the decision they were far enough in as she stopped.

"Yeah, we got it," replied Sean. He left the other two and headed deeper into the cemetery, blending in with the old oak trees and scattered bushes.

The sound of low voices came from the rear.

"I hope that's Riley and the boys," Matt said in a nervous whisper.

"Yeah, me too," replied Jenny.

Riley and two other boys climbed over the fence and moved through the dark toward Matt and Jenny.

"So, here we are. Where's the ghosts?" Riley asked. "Hey, where's the Yankee boy?" he chided.

"His grandma got sick so he couldn't come," Jenny said quickly.

"Yeah, I bet. He's just scared."

Matt said, "Let's move farther in and see if we can spot something."

They started forward, moving among the old tombstones.

Suddenly, a bush to their left rustled, breaking the stillness of the stifling night.

"What was that?" one of Riley's friends asked.

Another turned and ran for the fence.

Before anyone could answer, something came crashing across the cemetery to their right front. Walter, having just been released from the cage by the hiding Sean, was simply heading home, but in the dark cemetery he was an unrecognizable moving shadow.

On cue, Matt yelled, "Look out!" and shined a flashlight straight ahead and six feet high, where two large red eyes glared back at the group. Something that looked like a shadow danced around the fiery sockets.

Riley yelled, "Crimany! Let's get outta here!"

He and the remaining boy vaulted the fence at a dead run and sprinted down the street.

Matt and Jenny broke into hysterical laughter. Sean stepped from behind a tree, rolling up a rope tied to the sheet that had been draped behind two taillight reflectors tacked head high to skinny trees.

"Man, those things looked just like real eyes, and you worked that sheet like a champ," Matt said.

A low moaning came from behind them.

"What was that?" Jenny asked in a whisper.

The moaning started again, louder and closer. Sean looked at Matt in the darkness.

"It weren't me," Matt said in response to Sean's accusing look.

"Grab that stuff and let's get outta here!" Sean directed.

They moved toward the fence. A loud crashing sound followed by another low moan came from behind them. The three jokesters broke into full sprints.

Sean's flashback of that night brought forth more laughter. He placed his hands on the fence to steady himself, but jerked back when a slight electric shock tickled his body.

Static electricity, he thought, but no longer laughing.

Suddenly, leaves directly in front of him started swirling, rising above the ground. He looked up to the treetops for signs of a breeze, but it was calm.

The twirling leaves started forming a larger circle, and he heard a sound, like someone taking in a soft breath. He held his breath, listening. Then he heard ... what? ... A sigh. Yes, something like a sigh.

Just as suddenly as it had started, the noise from the leaves stopped. It was calm and the cemetery was quiet again.

"My imagination is getting payback," he said aloud as he turned to start walking to the jail to meet Matt.

CHAPTER 6

Matt was relieved to see that Mr. Usina was not outside when he arrived at the jail, since he was nearly late again.

He parked The Beast and ran to the gift shop, where he found Heidi unpacking stacked boxes containing gift items.

"Don't worry, it won't be that bad," Heidi said, laughing when she noted the helmet was still perched on Matt's head.

Matt rolled his eyes, embarrassed when he realized he had left his helmet on. "Oh, sorry," he said, removing it.

Heidi laughed again. "Just put it behind the counter. You can pick it up when you finish your jail check, which you may as well go ahead and do because we can't do anything with this stuff until I get the price checks tomorrow."

"You sure?" Matt said, glad he could get his checks out of the way as a rehearsal for the tour he had promised Sean.

"Yeah. Go ahead."

Matt walked around the front corner of the jail, retracing his path from yesterday. He noted with a chuckle that the turn-of-the-century human bird cage hanging on display did not contain a prisoner today. Man, he thought, that must have been a bummer, being in that thing while everybody gawked at you.

He found more trash around the gallows area ... and felt more goose bumps. Moving quickly through his assigned areas, he found himself standing in the open doorway of the sheriff's office.

He had thought about yesterday's experience only briefly, feeling silly about his imagination, or over-imagination. He was surprised, though, that some jokester had not come forward, since he suspected he was being "broken in." But here he was again and nevertheless hesitant to enter.

He took a deep breath and in a melodramatic voice, stated to the empty room, "Go, I must." With this exclamation, he took a step forward.

But he could not enter.

Whenever he tried to do so, he felt a curious sensation. Almost like he was pressing against a person. When he tried to move forward, he felt opposition. Confused, he pushed himself forward to enter the room, but the opposition he met was unyielding.

For what seemed like an hour but in fact was only seconds, he worked to enter. The unseen obstacle left him powerless.

Matt retreated a step back and as he did so, he clearly heard a low, twangy voice say, "Scared little boy," followed by a strange, small giggle.

He took another step backward and swallowed hard. His stomach grew queasy.

When he was no longer deafened by the roar that was his heart, he tried to think rationally. His galloping heart finally slowed.

He thought, Those guys are playing another joke. That's got to be it.

He looked around with a shiver and steadied his nerves. He knew he had to go into that room.

Matt took another deep breath and stepped forward. Another step. Then another. He listened. Nothing. Without opposition this time, he crossed the office and entered the parlor. Uneventful. With a sigh of relief, he purposefully but quickly made his checks and darted back to the open doorway.

Stepping into the hallway to head upstairs, he caught the faint sound of that weird laugh again. He quickened his pace and clamored up the steel and concrete stairs.

Out of nowhere, air rushed past him, flowing through his hair and causing his shirt to flutter.

While terror may have bound some adults to the spot at this point, not so with a young, imaginative mind littered with youthful curiosity and adolescent male pride that refused to be the wrong end of a joke.

Amazingly, for a young lad of sixteen who had just had a less than normal experience, he continued on. Thoughts coursed through his almost frozen brain: Is this all an elaborate hoax? But two days in a row? If I'm being broken in, someone's doing a good job.

Perhaps out of a deep sense of responsibility, or more likely, mild shock, Matt found himself standing at the sheriff's bedroom door.

There isn't much to check here so maybe I'll just skip it and leave, he rationalized. No, it wouldn't be right.

He stepped into what had been the children's bedroom in the old days, only to be greeted by that strange girlish, or old woman cackle.

"OK, I'm not buying this. Where are you?" he said aloud.

"You like this other scared little boy," the voice said. The high-pitched, squeaky sound reminded him of the wicked witch in *The Wizard of Oz*.

Now bordering on panic, Matt stammered, "What ... other boy? Where are you?"

He saw movement on the floor a few feet from the bed. No, not movement, but ... something. An object, with shape, but clear, almost like a vapor. It began to take shape, still clear, or maybe bluish, wavy ... and gaining form.

Matt turned and bolted from the room, almost falling down the stairs. He ran to the exit door downstairs and flung it open with a bang.

Once outside, he stopped and bent over, gasping for air.

"What are you doing, dude?"

Matt jumped at the sound of Sean's voice.

"Jeez, man, what's wrong with you?" Sean said.

"Sean," Matt gasped.

Concerned for his friend, Sean touched Matt's arm. "What were you doing, dude, working out on the stairs? You're drenched."

Matt slowly regained his composure. He looked around, hoping there would be jail employees laughing at their joke, but there was only Sean.

"How 'bout that tour you promised, man? I'm psyched." Sean surveyed Matt again. "That is, if you're up to it."

Matt, deciding to say nothing until he figured things out, looked at his friend. "No tour today. Maybe tomorrow. Let's go." He glanced around. "I gotta get my helmet out of the gift shop. I'll meet you at the bike." Matt pointed in the direction of the parked Beast.

Sean looked at him, confused. "OK," he said.

CHAPTER 7

Sean watched Matt hurry toward the gift shop, then strolled over to the bike and dug the extra helmet out of the sidecar, wondering why Matt was acting so strange.

"That you, Sean?"

"Samuel! Good to see you again." Sean grabbed the hand of the elderly carriage driver who had pulled up beside him. "How you doing?"

"Doin' good. Doin' good. Whoa, Blackout," Samuel called in a soothing voice to his horse.

"I see that ol' horse is still gettin' around."

"Oh yeah. Me and ol' Blackout hauled lots of tourists around today."

Samuel was a small, wiry man of an indeterminate age. He had driven tourists around St. Augustine in a horse and carriage for as long as anyone could remember. He was one of Honeyman's best friends and had known Matt all of the boy's life, and Sean for the past few years as a result of the summer visits.

"Well, and there's young Matt. How you doin', boy." Samuel squinted his wrinkled eyes and peered at the approaching Matthew. "You look pale. Feelin' OK?"

"Oh yeah, I'm fine, Samuel. How 'bout you?" Matt replied in a more reassuring tone than he felt.

"Can't complain. Can't complain."

Matt could have predicted the response of the elderly man he regarded so highly. Never complained and always had a gentle, calming effect on people.

"Say, you boys in a hurry?"

"No, all the time in the world," Sean responded before Matt could speak.

"Well then, I wonder if two strong boys might be willing to climb up here and go 'round the corner to help ol' Samuel unload this big ol' trunk at Mr. Pacetti's house."

"You bet. No problem. Right, Matt?"

"Happy to help, Samuel," Matt said, already feeling better just being near both his friends.

After they were seated, Samuel clucked gently to the horse. Blackout didn't move.

"Now Blackout, soon as we drop this trunk off, we goin' to get your oats, so no need to get all uppity."

The horse turned to look at Samuel and started a slow walk as if he understood that a reward was in his future.

"Ol' goat. He gets more ornery every year. Some days I don't know who's driving who."

"Well, from where I'm sittin', I'd say Blackout's doing the driving, Samuel," Sean said with a laugh.

"I 'spect you right about that. Yes sir."

They turned right out of the jail parking lot and headed into the neighborhood located directly behind the Old Jail.

Matt studied the gallows as they moved past the rear of the complex. "Say, Samuel, you know all those stories around here 'bout places being haunted and ghosts everywhere? You believe any of that stuff?"

His question drew a quick glance from Sean.

Samuel looked at the Old Jail, then at Matt. "Why do you ask that? You seein' ghosts in that ol' place you been workin'?" The old man chuckled.

"Well, no," Matt responded too quickly. "I was wondering …. I mean, you know, all these places, and you've been here forever."

"Ain't been here forever yet, but all my life so far, anyway." He looked at Matt again. After a brief silence, Samuel said casually, "I heard things from time to time 'round these ol' streets."

"Like what?" Sean chimed in.

"Well, lots of things. Like jus' the other night, goin' by that ol' cemetery—"

"Tolomato!" Sean interjected.

"Yeah, Tolomato. Oldest cemetery around, you know. All kinda dead folks in there."

He clucked at Blackout, whose pace had slowed to a crawl.

"Come on now, you ol' goat. Anyway, me and ol' Blackout was going by that cemetery jus' before dark. It was real quiet. Everybody eatin' supper. Anyhow, all of a sudden like, I hears this awful moaning. Thought maybe somebody hurt, so I stopped. Next thing I know, some of them bushes in there starts shaking and I smell something terrible awful. Never smelt nuthin' like it. Then more of them bushes start rattlin' and I heard moaning again." He stopped talking and deftly flicked a yellow fly off Blackout's rear with the carriage whip.

"Well, what happened?" Matt asked.

"Ain't nuthin' happen. Ol' Blackout 'bout to go crazy and I ain't seen nobody hurt, so we jus' got on outta there."

Gazing at a small house on their left, Samuel said, "I sure do like that new porch Mrs. Ponce put on that place."

The boys, eager for more detail, exchanged glances.

"Well, Samuel, what do you think it was?" Matt asked when it became obvious Samuel was finished with his story.

"Ain't the first time I heard things in that ol' place. Other places, too," he added.

"What things? What do you think it was?" Matt asked again.

"Well, don't rightly know. Ol' Hattie says .... You know Miss Hattie, don't you?"

Matt added, "The old woman in Lincolnville. I know who she is, but I don't know her. Lot of people scared of her. All that witchcraft and stuff."

"Oh shoot, you see how some folks get when they don't know 'bout something. Ain't no need to be scared of Miss Hattie. She ain't no witch jus' 'cause she talks to them ol' spirits. I known her all my life. I know folks go to her to get rid of demons and such."

Samuel eyeballed the boys. "Anyway, ol' Hattie says most folks die and go on up to heaven ..." He lowered his voice and leaned toward the boys. "Or somewhere else. Then there's those don't go to either place. They stuck here with no body. Kinda like lost."

"Samuel, you don't believe all that," Sean said.

"Ain't saying I do, ain't saying I don't. Jus' telling you what Hattie says. She might be old and never went to school, but she's smart. Why, I know folks that said she told them 'bout stuff gone happen, it happened, jus' like ol' Hattie say. Tell you somethin' else." He squinted his eyes and almost in a whisper, said, "Ol' Hattie won't go near that graveyard. Says there's big evil there. Goes to any other cemetery, but not that Tolomato."

"What about the jail?" Matt asked.

"You mean ghosts? Oh, I 'spect if there's ghosts around, they bound to be some there, all them poor souls been through that place. Some of 'em hanged. Bound to be some caught in the middle. That is, if there is any ghosts to start with."

"So you don't believe in ghosts," Sean persisted.

"I believe there are lots of things ol' Samuel don't understand or know about. Don't know about ghosts." Samuel paused a moment, then added, "Now me, I only saw one ghost—or somethin'."

"Whadda you mean you only saw one ghost," Sean said.

Samuel looked at Matt. "Honeyman never told you 'bout that ghost feller caught the same fish as me?"

"Whaa—" Matt composed himself and looked at the old man. "No, he never told me. What fellow? You're pulling my leg."

"Swear on the Bible," Samuel said.

Matt knew that phrase spoken by Samuel meant whether there was a ghost or not, he told what he believed.

"Anyhow, me and Honeyman was fishing, farther south down the St. Johns River and I hung a big 'un. Whew, that thing was heavy. I fought that fish so long, Honeyman had to take my rod for a spell. Finally, we see that big ol' fish head, so I keep working him, gettin' him closer and closer, but every now and then he git so heavy, it seemed like someone pulling him back—fightin' against me almost.

"Pretty soon though, that ol' fish is close enough I can see my hook in the side of that big ol' thing's mouth. He bustin' that water, makin' one devil of a racket. Well sir, he sticks that big head up again, shakin' and carryin' on, thrashin' like ain't there gonna be no tomorrow, and on the other side of his mouth, I see another hook. Line goin' out opposite way from me, like somebody pullin' the other way." He clucked at Blackout. "Come on, horse, we never gone git this trunk situated, way you movin'."

"So you're saying there was somebody else working that fish too? Or he was still hung on a line and rod he jerked in," Matt said.

"Well, he was sho' still hung all right, and that line went right up to a big ol' heavy-looking pole. Maybe like one of them thick bamboo kind." He looked at Matt seriously. "Definitely a rod and line, but weren't no man holdin' that rod. No sir. Something like a man, but not a real man. Kinda shaped like a man 'cept all fuzzy and wavy. Almost see through 'em, but not quite ... sho' had hold of that rod, though. I yanked back on my rod, and when I did, I see that other rod bend, pulling that fish that-a-way and that thing holdin' it starts wavin' and flutterin' more. Yes sir, that was shore sumthin'." He shook his head from side to side, then glanced at the two boys again.

"I know all that don't hardly seem possible, but ask Honeyman and he'll tell you the same thing." He broke into a small laugh. "Honeyman was yellin' to beat all dickens, tellin' me 'Cut the line, cut the line.' "

"What did you do?" Sean asked.

"Well, I cut the line. Weren't 'bout to tangle with that feller, or whatever it was." He took on a reflective gaze. "Now, this is the real strange part. Honeyman found out later that folks live around that area talk about a feller there a few years before this, that was tryin' to catch a big fish. You know, *the* biggin', a lunker. Been tryin' for years. Then one day he catches him. The lunker. So big, it pulls him right on in the river and he goes wadin' on out there, fightin' that fish, but he won't let go. Well, pretty soon the water over his head and he's gone. They say nobody seen him since, 'cept every now and agin, some fisherman reports seeing sumthin' out in that river like a man working a fish, 'cept ain't no boat and way too deep for anybody to be wadin'. They think that feller me and Honeyman saw was him."

Neither boy spoke.

"Ask Honeyman. It's the truth, all right. Ask him 'bout that Indian, too," he added. "Whoa, Blackout."

They had arrived at Mr. Pacetti's, and the teenagers, not sure of what they had just heard, unloaded the trunk in silence.

50

CHAPTER 8

At dusk the next day, a middle-aged tourist couple strolled down the sidewalk which fronts the Tolomato Cemetery. The cemetery is fenced and locked and not open to the public. There is, however, an indentation in the short mortar wall where one may step to read the history displayed on a brass plate. The vantage point also offers an unobstructed view of several grave markers.

The couple diverted from the sidewalk to read the placard.

"Look how old this is, honey," noted the heavyset man upon reading the narrative. "And look at those grave markers. Bet there's some history there."

"Back up and take a picture of me," the woman said as she turned to face Grenada Street, her back to the cemetery wall.

"OK." The man fumbled with his digital camera while backing up for a wider shot.

"Whaaaat!" the woman exclaimed.

The man looked up from his camera to see his wife bent backward, as if being grabbed from behind.

The man said, "What are you doing ..." but stopped when he saw the look of distress on his wife's face.

"Something's pulling me!" she yelled, fear lacing her voice.

"What are you talking about?" He started toward her, but she was suddenly thrust forward and the resulting collision sent the man and his camera falling to the ground. At the same time, they were both pelted with leaves and twigs as if a giant blower had scattered the ground debris from the cemetery.

The man struggled to regain his feet, his wife tugging on him while shrieking.

A strong gust of wind blew more debris over the couple as the man exclaimed, "What the hell!"

His wife followed his gaze to the cemetery where what seemed like a thousand miniature lightning bolts danced around, accompanied by a foul smell that was so overwhelming the woman gagged.

For several moments they could not move or speak, so oppressive and unbelievable was the situation.

The man began to regain his senses just as the thing, appearing now as a myriad of electrical arcs, started to form into ... something. A low, snarling sound came from its hollow form.

"Let's get outta here!" he yelled, grabbing his wife's hand.

They bolted the few feet down the sidewalk and ran into the Old Drugstore.

"Call the police!" the man yelled at Lynn, who was explaining a display setup to Sean.

"Oh my goodness," Lynn exclaimed, fearing an accident had happened.

"There's something out there," the man blurted out, visibly shaking.

"Where? What happened?" Lynn said.

"Out there. The cemetery. Call the police," the man both demanded and pleaded.

"OK. OK. Calm down. Ray, bring some water," Lynn instructed one of her employees. "Sean, go have a look."

"Me. Well, I ..." Sean stopped on seeing Lynn's glance as she continued her attempt to calm the couple, and then went out the door.

This is too much, he thought. He moved with uncertainty toward the cemetery.

He approached the area ... and could see debris scattered over the walkway. His feet crunched on dry leaves and twigs as he approached the fence that held the placard.

His breath coming in rapid spurts, Sean peered into the cemetery, straining his eyes and ears, wondering what lurked beyond his vision.

To his relief he saw that it was still and quiet.

Breathing easier, he turned to go and stepped on a camera, jumping as he did so. He quickly bent and retrieved it, then headed back to the drugstore.

Sean entered to find the man saying, "What— you think I'm crazy? I know what we saw, and look at this trash all over us."

"No, no. Of course you're not crazy. I'm only saying it's an old cemetery, and it's easy to some- times let our imagination get away," Lynn said soothingly. "We have these little wind gusts all the time here near the bay. You just got caught in one."

"Lady, don't patronize me! I tell ..." He grappled with his words. "Oh, hell. Come on, hon, let's get out of here. I need a drink," he spit out with one last glaring look at Lynn.

"Is this your camera, mister?" Sean said as the couple turned to go.

The tourist jerked the camera from Sean's hand without speaking and stomped through the door-way, his dazed wife following close behind.

"Guess it is," Sean said. "Jeez. Tourists."

Lynn turned to Sean. "What did you see? A bunch of ghosts on the loose?"

"No. Just a bunch of trash. Whadda you think they saw?"

"That place is haunted," Ray said, "that's what it is."

"Oh crap, Ray. Don't start that again," Lynn said, rolling her eyes.

She turned to Sean. "Happens every now and then, son. Tourists let their imagination get away from 'em. Don't worry about it." She turned away and looked back over her shoulder. "Oh, and get the broom and dustpan and get those leaves up, will you, hon? Then you can go ahead and take off."

Sean completed his chore and stepped out the front door to find Ray talking to Jenny on the drugstore deck.

"Hey. Ray told me what happened. That's really weird." She placed her hands on her hips and cocked her head slightly. "You see any ghosts?"

"No, I didn't see any ghosts," he retorted too quickly. "I guess you have, huh?"

"Don't be silly, Yankee boy." She looked at Sean suspiciously. "You act like you're not sure."

"No, I was just asking. What are you doing here, anyway?"

"Well, you two carry on if you want to, but lots of people I know and heard about seen strange things in the Ol' Town," Ray said. The Minorcan descendant gave the teens a serious look. "I been in this town all my life, family here for generations, and I heard lots of stories about encounters that can't be explained." He shifted his gaze to the cemetery. "And that place," he added, shaking his head, "that place probably got the most stories. Heard things there myself—more 'n once." He looked at Jenny. "You from here. You mean to tell me you never heard any of those old stories?"

"Well yeah, I guess, some."

"You think with all those stories, and people carry'n on, ain't nothing to any of 'em?"

"Well, I hadn't—"

"I'm simply saying look around you. Pay attention before you go pooh-poohing something just because you ain't seen it." He turned and stomped into the building.

"Wow, I think Ray's been working next to that cemetery too long." She looked at Sean. "Anyway, I came by to see how you were doing with the job." She smiled knowingly. "Looks like it has been a little exciting."

"Yeah. It's OK. I like it fine." He glanced toward the cemetery. "Kinda strange working next to a graveyard, I guess."

"Now, don't tell me the big-city boy is getting spooked about a graveyard. You sound like Ray."

"I didn't say that! I said it was weird. Jeez, don't make a big deal of it."

"Well, 'scuse me. You sure are testy."

"No. No. I didn't mean ... well, anyway, I'm not mad at you, Jen-girl. Things are moving so fast, I guess."

"I forgive you." She flashed a big smile. "If you're through for the day, I might even give you a ride home."

"Uh, I'm done, but no thanks," Sean replied, staring at the pink flamingo parked by the deck.

"Besides," he added, "I told Matt I'd meet him at the jail. He's gonna give me the tour. Private, no less."

"That's even better. Come on, I'll give you a ride to the jail. I want to see the act, too."

"Well, I don't know if Matt could handle that. He seems to get a little confused around the Jen-girl these days."

"Don't be silly," she replied, blushing.

Sean watched her with a big grin on his face. As the older of the three teenagers, he sometimes savored the "sage" role.

"Anyway, I'm not getting on that thing." He let Jenny off the hook and eyeballed the moped. "Why in the world did you get pink, anyway? And who drew the flowers on the fenders?"

"I did. Looks cool, huh?"

"Oh yes, it's quite lovely. But I ain't gettin' on it."

"OK. It's perfectly all right. I understand if you're not comfortable with your sense of masculinity." She sashayed toward the bike.

Sean rolled his eyes. "I see you're still reading all that psychology stuff. Besides, you ain't got but one helmet."

"It's 'You don't have but one helmet,' dummy," she said, pulling an extra helmet from the small rear box compartment. "And this might fit your big head. *And,*" she added, "it will camouflage your face so none of your many admirers will recognize you, therefore saving you from any injury to your male pride."

She began putting her helmet on, after placing the extra one on the rear seat.

Without speaking, Sean stomped to the bike and grabbed the helmet.

"And don't forget I'm the driver, so keep your comments to yourself. And hold on, but not too tight."

She cranked the small bike as Sean took a worried glance around.

CHAPTER 9

Matt was sprawled on one of the trolley stop benches in front of the jail when he saw the moped pull into the parking lot.

He had expected Sean to be walking alone and was surprised, and maybe a little jealous, to see him hanging on to Jenny as the bike moved toward him.

"I never thought I'd say it, but I think I prefer your Beast's sidecar," Sean said to him as he dismounted the small bike in dramatic fashion. "The Jen-girl wanted to hear your tour pitch, too."

Noting Matt's accusing look, he quickly added, "She stopped by the drugstore to see Lynn, and I bummed a ride."

"That's right." Jenny did not correct Sean's modified story. "You won't believe what happened. Sean had his first major tourist encounter."

"What does that mean?" Matt said, still uncomfortable with the situation.

"That cemetery next to the drugstore— Tolomato? ..."

"I know the name of the cemetery."

"Well, I hope you do. Remember a few years back when we got Riley and the boys," she said, trying to lighten Matt's demeanor.

"Are you gonna tell me what happened or not?"

Jenny pondered Matt's comment. "Sean, you tell him. You were the one there anyway, and maybe Mr. Impatient here won't keep interrupting you." She sat down on the opposite end of the bench from Matt.

"I've heard a thousand tourist stories already," Matt said.

"Not like this one." Sean, tired of their sparring match, said, "Two tourists said they got accosted by spooks in front of the cemetery."

"What? Are you serious? What happened?"

"You sure you're interested? I don't want to waste my energy if you're gonna keep acting like a chump."

Matt looked at Sean, then glanced at Jenny, who was pouting at the other end of the bench. He laughed. "Guess I was, huh? Thanks for pointing that out. Sorry, Jen."

"OK," Jenny said. "Now that we're back to normal, tell him."

For several minutes Sean regaled them with his recollection of the event, with brief interruptions from Matt and Jenny to clarify points.

Sean finished and moved to sit down on the bench. "Move down, Jen-girl, I need a rest now." He gestured Jenny toward Matt.

Jenny slid closer to Matt than necessary, after an understanding glance at Sean.

Matt was oblivious to the move. He said, "So you really didn't see anything?"

"No, I didn't see what they saw, but like I said, they had trash all over them, and the guy had dropped his camera."

"So you believe 'em?"

Sean thought about his own experience. "Well, they were definitely shaken. The woman could hardly talk."

"Ray must have believed them. He gave us a lecture on ghosts in the Old Town," Jenny said.

"I know Ray. He's from a really old St. Augustine family. Good guy." Matt paused. "So Ray thought there was something to it, huh?"

"Guess he did. Accused the Jen-girl and me of pooh-poohing everything."

"Well, maybe you shouldn't—"

"Matt." Mr. Usina came walking up. "You're off the hook tonight."

"Sir?"

"Got a visiting VIP group coming over for a private tour, so I have to take them through. Last-minute thing. You and your friends can tag along if you like."

A large tour bus rolled into the parking lot before Matt could answer.

"Oh, here they are. If you guys wanna go, just go on over to the rear door. I gotta get these folks organized." He hurried toward the bus.

"OK, Mr. Usina. Thanks." Matt was relieved because he was nervous about giving his tour narrative with the unexpected Jenny present.

"Oh well," he said to the other two. "What do you guys want to do?"

"I wanted to hear you do it, dude."

"Me too," Jenny echoed.

"Well then, won't be today. We have all summer, anyway."

Jenny said, "Let's go over to Dunkin' Donuts. I'm buying."

"Hey, let's saddle up." Sean started walking toward The Beast.

"Sounds good." Matt stood to follow, but Jenny touched his arm.

"Matt, I'm sorry I upset you earlier. I didn't intend to."

"Oh, no. You didn't. It was me just being a twit. I'm the one that's sorry."

"You're not a twit. You're sweet." She squeezed his arm. "Like that donut I can already taste."

Sean yelled out, "You guys coming or what? I can't wait for another ride in this contraption."

"Oh, which reminds me," Matt said, regaining his senses. "You want to go to Honeyman's tomorrow? He called, said he got the new fender for The Beast and we're gonna put it on."

"Definitely. I want to see Honeyman, anyway. Think he might have some of that river grub on hand?"

"You know Honeyman."

"Oh yeah. I'm there. Let's get the donuts. I suddenly got hungry.

CHAPTER 10

With some apprehension, Matt released the clutch of The Beast and moved cautiously across U.S. Highway 1 on King Street. Even at seven thirty in the morning, the highway was very busy, but once across, it would be light traffic and clear sailing on King Street all the way to the dead-end intersection with Highway 13 on the St. Johns River. Because of few crossroads and minimum traffic, this was the only route to Honeyman's that Matt was allowed to use with The Beast. That suited him because it was a really nice drive through open farmlands and woodlands and eventually, the scenic ride on 13 alongside the river.

Sean was nestled in the sidecar finishing the egg sandwich he had run out with while munching when Matt had blown the horn for him to depart moments ago.

After about fifteen minutes, they stopped at Highway 13 and turned right, riding along the river road.

"Hey, remember this little pond?" Matt yelled at Sean over the noisy motor.

"Yeah, yeah, yeah. St. Johns River. Three hundred ten miles long, runs South to North, which is backward, and empties into the Atlantic Ocean."

Matt grinned into the wind at Sean's response, noting with satisfaction there were no other vehicles in sight on the narrow road. He would have chosen this route to Honeyman's even if his dad had not imposed the rule.

Seeing a squirrel dart into the roadway several feet ahead, Matt gradually applied the brakes of the old bike.

Sean asked, "Why don't you just swing around him?"

While Sean spoke, the squirrel stopped in the center of the road, jumped up several inches, turned, ran back the same way he had come and scurried up a tree.

"Now you know why." Matt grinned. "You never know which way they're gonna go. Can't figure that one out."

He deftly shifted the foot gear and accelerated back up to the 45-mile-per-hour speed limit.

A few minutes later they turned into Honeyman's yard and pulled into the cypress board garage where Matt could see tools already in place for the fender project.

"You boys had breakfast yet?" Honeyman called to them from the front porch.

"Sean ate all the way out here."

"And I could still eat," Sean responded to Matt's jest, remembering Honeyman's famous pancakes.

"Kinda figured that, so I put together some extra pancake batter. Got a couple leftover cats, too. Come on in." He gave each of the boys a hug. "Good to see you again, Sean. How are you?"

"I'm good, Honeyman. It's really great to see you too. Did you say catfish?" Sean quipped as they all laughed, recalling Sean's discovery of southern-fried catfish during his first visit. He had to be persuaded to taste the local delicacy, only to evolve into an impressive all-you-can-eater down at the Crab Shack.

"You boys sit down and let's see if we can fill you up. That ol' fender won't take no time to get on." Honeyman spooned batter into his all-purpose cast-iron pan, then placed an already cooked plate of catfish in the still warm oven. "We'll stick these in here to keep 'em warm," he said with a wink at Matt.

Matt knew they weren't leftovers at all, rightly suspecting that Honeyman cooked them up for their visit, knowing Sean's appetite and partiality to the river critter.

Soon the boys were enjoying pancakes so light they almost floated off the plate. Sean was munching on his third cat.

"I don't know as I ever seen a boy could eat like you, Sean. Reminds me of ol' Samuel when he was young. Wheweee! That fool could eat." Honeyman laughed.

"Oh yeah," Matt said over a mouthful of pancake, "we saw Samuel a couple days ago. Said to tell you hello."

"He doin' good?" Honeyman asked, concerned.

"Same ol' Samuel. Drivin' that carriage, you know."

"Best friend a man ever had," Honeyman said fondly about his friend of more than sixty years. "Wish he'd quit that carriage stuff. At least when it's so hot. He's too old for that anymore." He sounded worried.

Matt smiled at Honeyman's reference to Samuel as old, since his grandfather was slightly older. "Honeyman, you know he's never gonna do that."

"Yeah, I know. They'll probably find him in that carriage after his soul done gone to heaven."

The boys exchanged glances, obviously thinking the same thing.

Matt spoke first. "He told us about that fish thing."

"Yeah, did you guys really see a fisherman ghost? Samuel swears you did," Sean said before Honeyman could respond.

Honeyman appeared to be in thought, and then grunted. "Well, guess I'm surprised at Samuel. We usually keep that to ourselves." He paused, then added, "You know how people are 'bout stuff like that."

"So you did see it?" Matt asked.

"Oh yeah, we saw something."

No one spoke for several seconds. The boys exchanged looks, played with their food, as if waiting for more.

Honeyman picked up on the teens' demeanor. "You boys got something else on your mind? No need for me to repeat Samuel's story. We saw what we saw."

"So, Honeyman, you believe in ghosts," Sean said as more of a statement than question.

"Well, I believe what me and ol' Samuel saw weren't hardly alive; least not like you and me," he stated with conviction. "Ain't the strangest thing I ever saw, though." He poured another cup of coffee.

"You mean the Indian thing?" Sean asked.

Honeyman set his cup down. "You mean Samuel told you about my run-in with that ol' chief? That ol' fool shore talking a lot lately."

"Oh no, Honeyman. He didn't really tell us anything," Matt said, defending Samuel. "He just said to ask you about it."

He watched Honeyman pour coffee into his saucer to cool it, then sip it with obvious pleasure, the old-fashioned way.

"Guess he figured you'd tell us if you wanted to," Matt added.

Honeyman smiled, thinking his grandson was becoming wise in persuasive tactics. He seemed to contemplate the coffee in his saucer, and then glanced at the boys' plates. "You boys want some more 'cakes or fish?"

"No. No. I'm full," they both responded, causing him to smile.

"Well, guess we ought to let our breakfast settle a little before we tackle that fender." Another sip from the deep saucer. "May as well tell you boys that story while we're waitin'. If you think you want to hear about it."

The identical reply: "We wanna hear it."

"Well, it was a long time ago," he started, leaning back comfortably in the deep blue wood-frame chair. "I was a young man, not much older than you two boys. We did all kind of things in them days to make a living. I ran trot lines, hunted gators, grew stuff and sold it, you know, such as that." He stared thoughtfully out the window, a distant look in his eyes as he recalled times past.

"I was also tryin' to build myself a herd of cows. Finally had 'bout seven or eight head, woods cows—kinda take care of themselves, you know— over there on Jack Wright Island." He gestured out the kitchen toward the other side of the river. "Let 'em roam the swamps there foraging. Lots of folks did that then with cows and hogs.

"Now, one of them Pacetti boys had an old, broken Model A Ford truck I wanted, and he said I could have it for one of my cows. Well, that suited me, so off I went to round them cows up so's I could pick out which one to give 'em. Wanted to make sure I got a good 'un, 'cause I shore wanted that truck. Right thing to do anyway.

"Me and that sorry ol' dog of mine, Murphy, went tromping down through the swamp and 'fore long, it started getting' a little muddy and the cypress trees got bigger, so I knew I must be close to Trout Creek. Figured wouldn't be no cows that far in 'cause it was so wet, so I decided I'd circle back around.

"Well sir, as I started off to my right, by a giant cypress tree—biggest thing I ever seen—I could see something on the ground 'bout twenty feet away.

"I made my way through the thick brush and I could see that it was like a big hump on the ground. Couldn't see it good though, all them palmettos and such, but figured it might be a cow down, stuck in the mud, you know.

"I was finally about eight or ten feet from whatever it was, but I could see it weren't no cow. I could tell that. Anyhow, I eased closer, but something didn't seem right. Just felt kinda strange. I had to shush ol' Murphy—fool was growlin' and takin' on. Then it hit me what was wrong. It was quiet. Dead quiet. Now, you know there's always a lot of noise in them swamps; all kinds of bugs, frogs, birds and such. The swamp noisy all the time. So this situation was real strange.

"Now, it was strange, like I said, but I didn't think nuthin' more 'bout it and moved closer to the thing on the ground. I could now see that it was maybe three feet high, 'bout six, seven feet long and might be a gator nest." He paused, then continued.

"Anyway, I figured if it was a nest, I'd get me some eggs to hatch out and sell, so I leaned my shotgun against the end of the mound and started clearing off some of the trash with a stick. All kind of leaves, sticks, cypress moss and such on it, so I was keepin' a sharp eye out for snakes.

"I figured out pretty quick it weren't no gator nest, so I keep clearing stuff away to have a better look. Right then, my shotgun fell over and that sorry dog started growling again.

"Then it occurred to me that this might be an old Indian mound. I had seen a couple before, but they were all tore up and weren't very big. I was thinking if this was a mound, it shore looked like it had never been messed with.

"All of a sudden-like, my gun that had fell down scooted across the ground like somebody kicked it.

"Now, ol' Murphy was still standing 'bout six feet behind me, and he starts growlin' again to beat all dickens. I reached to pick up my gun, and when I did, the leaves and stuff on top of that mound started movin' and cracklin'. You could hear it good because it was still dead quiet. No sound at all 'cept the racket all that stuff was making. Then them leaves start goin' up like somebody was sucking them up with a vacuum cleaner. Well sir, I don't mind tellin' you, I moved back a little more.

"Now as I kept backing up a little, something started oozing up with them leaves. All mixed in together. I thought it was swamp gas, but it started taking on a shape, kinda like a man. I couldn't hardly move 'cause I never seen nothing like it. It was like a man, big man, maybe near seven feet, but it was kinda whitish, maybe blue, and wavy, but seemed like I could see right through it. It was kinda like—"

"Liquid, like water. Floaty!" Sean blurted out, then caught himself.

"Well, yeah, guess it was, 'bout like you said." Honeyman eyed Sean curiously.

"Murphy yelped and took off. I was 'bout to do the same when I see what looked like an arm on this thing reach down to the mound and come back up with something in what I guess was its hand. Now this thing in his hand was not milky or wavy-looking like that thing was. It looked real and it looked like a hatchet.

"The thing raised it over his head, like you do if you was gonna throw a hatchet." He stopped talking. Thoughtfully, he stared out the window. He finally said, "I can see it like it was yesterday."

"What happened?" Sean almost whispered.

"What happened was I turned and hightailed it back the way I come. I spotted that big ol' cypress tree that I had made my marker so's not to get lost,—that, and a big boulder close by it—and I headed for it, lickety split.

"Just before I made that tree, 'bout twenty feet from the mound, all them cypress knots tripped me up and I fell right at the base of that tree." He eyed the boys grimly. "Then I hear somethin' hit that tree right above my head.

"I looked up and right there stuck in that ol' cypress was a tomahawk, or war ax, or somethin' like one. I couldn't inspect it too close 'cause I was up and runnin' for all I was worth and I didn't stop till I was well out of them swamps."

"No way! Whadda you think it was?" Matt exclaimed, almost breathless.

"Like I said, somethin' like a tomahawk ..."

"No, I mean that thing—that thing you saw," Matt clarified.

"Oh, well, this is the really strange thing. I went on 'bout my business. Didn't say nothin' 'bout it to nobody 'cause they would have put me away in those days. Then, musta been three or four weeks later, I stopped at ol' man Mosely's store to pick up some supplies, and him and a bunch of fellers was talkin' on the porch. City boys, I could tell. Anyhow,

I went on in and started gatherin' my supplies. Mosely came in after a spell, laughin' like they's no tomorrow. 'Those fellers from that college over in Gainesville. Been here a week or so and you know why?' he asked me.

" 'No. Reckon I don't.'

" 'Well, they's some of them history boys like to dig things up. You know what I mean?'

" 'Yeah, I guess so.'

" 'Anyhow, they been pokin' 'round looking for Injun stuff, you know, graves and such. Been talking to folks wantin' to know if anybody ever hear any old stories 'bout one of them Timucua Injun chiefs. Said that feller might have had something that when he drank from it, he got real mean. Said the Indians called it tinaja—that's their word for something to drink out of, only this one had some kind of magic power. These college boys said the sign of this chief feller was a small feather. Carved it on his stuff and none of those other Injuns could use that sign. Them boys said they figured out he might be buried somewhere around here.' "

Honeyman stood up and stretched. "Well, that's it, boys. You two are the only ones I ever told 'cept for Samuel. Now, I won't tell ya'll not to tell anybody, but if you do, be careful, 'cause lot of people don't respect or believe what they ain't seen themselves, and that can be aggravatin'—and cause some folks to look at you funny. I told you boys 'cause I think you do respect that I wouldn't tell you a bald-faced lie."

The boys exchanged glances, mesmerized by the story.

"That's something," Sean said, breaking the silence.

"Did you ever go back?" Matt asked.

"Never."

"You think it's still there?" Sean asked as he leaned forward.

Honeyman could tell what was coming next.

"Well, good chance it is 'cause nobody goes that deep in the swamp. No need to. Can't get to the creek to fish—too wet and muddy. Can't hunt 'cause it's too thick to shoot. Besides, that area been under wetland rules for years, so can't nobody do nothing back there." He paused and eyeballed the boys. "Yeah, it's probably still there. Be hard to find, though, it'd be so overgrown."

He gave them both another look.

"Boys, I 'spect I know what you're thinking and the answer is no, I can't take you there. Whatever I saw was buried there, and evil or not, he's got a right to rest without folks pokin' 'round. Somebody thought enough of that feller to put him there, so we need to let him be. You understand?"

"Yes, sir," they said in harmony, a note of disappointment in their voices.

"Good. OK then, let's get that new fender on the ol' Indian." He turned and smiled. "The one with the motor, that is."

After the boys left, Honeyman went out to his dock to enjoy the warm, pleasant breeze coming off his river. It had been years since he had thought about the Indian mound and his experience. Now, staring across the narrow part of the river between his place and Jack Wright Island, he found that telling the story had rekindled his curiosity.

With a grunt, he stood up from his rickety dock chair and walked straight to his truck.

Thoughts of a long time past pushed to the forefront and he headed toward Jack Wright Island. He remembered when it took him more than an hour to get there by horse. Now, fifteen minutes later in the truck, he pulled off Highway 13 and turned down a dark trail that soon ended at a thickening swamp.

He took a machete from the rear of his truck and began making his way through the trees and brush, stopping every few feet to recollect and get his bearings.

Soon he spotted the big, smooth boulder he remembered from years before, and perhaps sixty feet ahead of it, what had to be the huge cypress tree. He headed toward it.

The ground became wetter and muddier, and soon his shoes and coverall bottoms were soaked.

Honeyman stopped to catch his breath and wiped sweat from his eyes with the back of his hand. He felt foolish for being out here alone, but he was not afraid.

When he reached the giant tree, Honeyman looked it over, starting at the base and working his way up.

Immediately below his eye level he could see where the tree had grown over something. He could tell it was a hatchet-like object, the handle missing—probably had been wood, and rotted away, he surmised.

He wiped his glasses with a red handkerchief he always carried and studied the deeply embedded hatchet head. Soon, he speculated, it would be totally consumed by the tree growing around it.

Honeyman rubbed the slightly exposed part of the object and could make out some sort of etching. Maybe part of a feather. Maybe not. He looked toward where he remembered the mound to be, but it was now so thick and heavily treed, he could see nothing but thick growth.

He thought about moving closer but knew it could serve no purpose.

His eyes traveled from the mound, up the tall trees silhouetted against the late afternoon sky in solemn grandeur.

From somewhere deep in the swamp he heard the reptilian growl of a blue heron.

With a wry smile, he turned to make his way back to his truck. "Guess I'd be upset too, if some fool started messin' with my grave," he said aloud.

CHAPTER 11

"Hurry up, man. I'm gonna be late. Again!"

Matt urged Sean as the latter struggled to climb out of the tight sidecar. The river trip had taken longer than expected, so as Matt turned into the drugstore to drop him for work, he advised Sean to be quick.

"OK, OK," Sean responded, finally freeing himself, only to fall in a heap.

"You OK?" Matt felt bad that he had hurried his friend.

"I'm cool. Go ahead."

Matt shook his head and roared off.

Sean reported to Lynn and was advised he would be bussing tables in the café.

After three hours of stacking dirty dishes and listening to the chatter of tourists, he was happy to be performing his last chore—crushing all the boxes and lugging them to the trash bin.

The soft dusk breeze was refreshing compared to the hot café kitchen. He avoided looking into the cemetery as he threw the last box in, and turned to head home for dinner with his grandmother.

A buzzing noise caught his ear, and his eyes followed the sound to the halogen security light located at the corner of the cemetery fence.

The noise grew louder and the light began to grow brightly. He watched the glow intensify until finally, in a shower of sparks, it blew out.

In the silent aftermath of the loud buzzing, the breeze had stopped and it was very still.

Willing himself to leave, he instead turned and looked into the cemetery.

Daylight was fading and the graveyard was swallowed up by the encroaching night. A stinging numbness began in his nerve endings. A feeling of dread swept over him.

As if being drawn by some invisible force, he walked the four feet to the fence.

In disbelief, he watched a moving vapor-like thing come toward him. ... The pale blue, almost white mist gathered form, moving closer to him.

The form took on human shape but was barely recognizable as such. He heard a sigh as it drew near.

"Be careful." The voice, like a young boy's, came from the form, which appeared to waver with the sound it uttered.

Suddenly the trees and bushes to the right of the form shook violently and ground debris swirled toward the shape. Its flowing mass seemed to quiver.

"Run," the voice urged, just as a dead tree limb was seemingly hurled at the form, causing it to fade away into the darkness.

Sean was torn from his disbelieving trance when something like hot, rank breath caught him full in the face.

He heard a low snarl as he turned and ran gagging across the parking lot.

CHAPTER 12

Sean's mind was whirling as he walked from the drugstore to his grandmother's house.

"Oh man!" he said aloud when he realized he was looking around for spooks, or whatever, at every step.

He arrived home and felt a surge of relief.

"Hope you're hungry, Sean," Mrs. Kirk said, greeting him.

"Starved," he replied, though in fact he felt the opposite. His experience had been so intense, he still felt nauseated.

He joined his grandmother at the table after a quick wash.

"Looks great, Grandma."

"Oh, I hope it is. Just got those squash out of Maria Masters' garden this afternoon. Which reminds me, I'd like you and Sean to go to Maria's with me one day this week to move that big ol' couch of hers."

"Sure thing, Grandma." Sean picked at his food.

"Something wrong, son? You've hardly eaten anything."

"Oh, no. It's great," he replied, forcing himself to eat the food.

Mrs. Kirk reached across the table and gripped the top of Sean's hand with a brief squeeze and continued holding it with a gentle touch.

"I'm so glad you came again this summer. I enjoy your visits so much."

Sean looked up at the lady he had grown to love so much. Though he liked New York, he sometimes found himself wishing he could live here with his grandmother. He felt as if she knew what he was thinking. Only recently did he realize that she had helped him resolve many adolescent issues without his even being aware of her guiding hand.

He finally said, "Not nearly as much as I do."

She gave his hand a final squeeze and returned to her plate.

Sean watched her as she chattered about various things. He tried to show interest, but his mind kept wandering back to the cemetery.

"Grandma, can I ask you something?" Sean said without thinking, interrupting her review of today's newspaper article announcing the various July Fourth celebration events a few days away.

"Well, of course you can, honey. You know you can always ask me anything."

Sean knew that to be true.

"Well, I was wondering ... you know, how you have lived in this Old Town for so long." He hesitated and gave her a quick look.

"I have lived here my whole life. Right here in this house since I was not much younger than you," she quickly said, sensing his reluctance to speak openly. "Something about the Old Town you want to know?"

Sean took in a deep breath. "Well, I was just wondering about all this ghost stuff. You know, all these places supposed to be haunted and all."

She chuckled in a reassuring manner. "Well, we sure got enough ghost tours, so must be ghosts somewhere." She studied the boy's reaction, not wanting to sound patronizing. "But I don't know how much of that stuff is true."

"But what do you think? I mean about ghosts and stuff."

"I guess I think there are a lot of things none of us understand." She leaned back in her chair, contemplating the boy staring at his plate, toying with his food.

Neither spoke.

The old lady had a feeling her grandson's question was driven by more than a passing curiosity. Being elderly has its merits and certainly one is having the wisdom to not confront young folks directly when they seem reluctant to talk.

"You know, I can't tell you how many times I've thought about this over the years, but I guess I have to say that I probably saw a ghost, or something, once."

Sean's head shot up. "What! Where? When?" His reaction to his grandmother's statement was a relief that maybe he wasn't imagining things, and excited his curiosity to learn more.

"I've never told but two other people what I saw. One of those, Jake Colee, bless his soul, actually then told me his own story about what I saw. Even your dad doesn't know."

"Will you tell me?" Sean asked, almost pleading.

"I will, yes." She put a finger to her lips. "But you must not tell any others." She leaned forward. "Least till I'm long gone. Don't want folks around here looking at me crazy."

She smiled.

"I promise. Tell the story."

"Come on." She stood up and moved to her easy chair. "Let's sit over here."

Sean followed and they settled down.

"We moved into this house when I was near your age," she began. "Now, when Grandpa and I married a few years later, I moved over 'cross town, but when my folks died, I got Grandpa to move back." She looked around. "I love this grand old house.

"Anyway, my folks bought this house sudden-like. Seems a young lady who lived here with her parents died, and they were so grief stricken, they wanted to leave right away. So we bought it because it's bigger and has that wonderful garden out back."

Sean shifted in his chair, anxious to hear about ghosts, not family history. The old lady peered at him over her glasses and smiled.

"Anyway, Jake Colee was very old at the time and he kinda came with the house. He was the family gardener, handyman and about everything else, and lived in that little cottage back there. Poor soul didn't have anywhere else to go, so Papa let him stay. I grew to love him like a second father."

She shook her head.

"We were here scarcely a few weeks when one evening in my upstairs bedroom, I looked out into the garden and saw, among the rose bushes, a figure in what seemed to be a flowing dress. On closer look, I could see that it was not a person at all. Well, not like us, and it was moving slightly above the ground, headin' toward the garden trellis.

"Now, you know I was more than a little scared, but I could not leave the window. It was incredible to me. The figure kept moving, flowing, almost liquid-like, with a slight whitish glow, and something sparkled around its neck.

"Then I saw something move to my left, around the trellis. It was another figure, except instead of something like a flowing gown, it looked more defined in shape and, perhaps, masculine.

"The two moved toward each other as slender, wavy forms raised up from each, until they merged together."

She grew silent and sat dream-eyed, a slight smile on her face.

"Grandma, what happened then?"

"Oh, well, I saw the same thing on two other occasions, always moving toward each other in the same area. I think those wavy, slender things reaching out were arms lifted to embrace."

She searched Sean's face for a reaction, but he sat, mouth open, waiting for her to continue.

"The third time I saw them, I decided to confide in someone, so I told Jake Colee, who had by then become my good friend, and since he lived in that garden cottage, I thought maybe he might have seen something.

"The first thing he said was, 'Was one wearing a broach at her neck?' I realized, of course, that the sparkle I saw could have been a broach, so I said, 'Yes, I think so.'

"He took my hand and said, 'Don't worry, Miss Karen. That was just Edward and Susan. They won't hurt you.'

"Then he told me this story: In this house back then lived a lovely young lady named Susan, with her parents and sister. They were a family of means—you know, financially comfortable.

"Susan had many admirers, but Edward was the one she fancied. Her father forbade the relationship, not impressed with Edward's station in life.

"They continued to see each other secretly in the garden. Edward arrived for one of those rendezvous to find Susan being molested by another young suitor, the son of a prominent family. The men fought, and Edward killed the molester.

"Because of his status, Edward knew he would surely be put to death for his crime, though it was self-defense. Susan agreed he must flee. Edward presented her with a cameo broach. He kissed her goodbye with a promise to send for her once he was settled somewhere else.

"A year passed, and no word came from Edward. In spite of her father's urging, she turned down all other suitors and began to suffer ill health until finally she died from heartbreak over her lost love. Unaware her father had withheld Edward's letters, the last words she mumbled were 'Why did you forsake me, Edward?' "

The old woman's eyes were moist. She dabbed at them with her handkerchief, sniffed graciously and continued.

"Jake Colee was close to the family, so he agreed to cover Susan's grave after the funeral three days later. All the mourners left and poor ol' Jake started his chore. Said it was the hardest thing he ever had to do—she was such a sweet girl. Well, he threw in a shovelful of dirt and a sound came from the open grave. Like a deep sigh. The wind, he thought. But then there was another sigh, followed by a voice, clearly Susan's, that said, 'Oh Edward, why have you forsaken me? Can I never rest?'

"Jake told me he would have run but for his deep affection for Susan and the family.

"As he once again began filling the grave, Edward appeared, looking very tired and worn.

"He stopped Jake's digging, yelling 'She called to me three days ago, asking why I had forsaken her. I must tell her I did not. Open the coffin,' he demanded of Jake.

"Jake could not reason with the poor man, so reluctantly, he pried the lid open.

"Edward fell to his knees and kissed the dead woman, vowing that he had not forsaken her and would rest with her soon.

"That very day, Edward turned himself in to the sheriff, for he was still a wanted man. After being sentenced to hang, he smiled all the way up the steps of the gallows." Mrs. Kirk leaned forward. "Right over at that Ol' Jail where Matt works. When Sheriff Joe asked if he had any last words, he just said, 'Now we will be together forever.'

"Now, Edward could not be buried in that cemetery because he did, after all, kill a man, so Jake was afraid dear Susan would still not be at rest. But he returned to the cemetery several times, and never again heard anything from the grave.

93

"This he took to mean she was at rest, and when I told him of my encounters, he said they were finally together."

Mrs. Kirk sat back with her eyes closed, exhausted from her story.

"Grandma, do you believe that story? It's like a weird love story."

"Oh Sean, I don't know about weird, but it is a love story," she replied, not opening her eyes. "I saw something very unusual, very different. I truly did." She opened her eyes and looked at the young boy with a soft but challenging expression.

"If I had not seen what I know was that young couple, I don't know whether or not I would have believed Jake's story, even as much as I loved him. But I did see them, and things I learned later confirmed to me that Jake was telling the truth. Now, were they ghosts? I don't know, but they weren't like you and me, and they could feel. They reached for each other. I could sense their feelings—still can, even now, after all these years." She rested her white head on the chair back and stared up at the ceiling with a smile.

"I don't know, Grandma ..." Sean started, then recalled his own experience, "but I do believe you."

She reached out and took his hand.

In a soft whisper she said, "I'm glad, son. I'm glad."

CHAPTER 13

The next day brought clear blue skies, and the water off Vilano Beach was particularly green.

Sean and Matt sat in the sand watching Jenny pick through shells several feet away. Her fashionably pink swimsuit was prominent against the background of the calm Atlantic surf.

Her movements were graceful; she stooped to pick up a shell, examined it closely and then placed it in a net bag. Jenny was athletic and tanned, so it was no surprise that each boy who passed her did a double-take, acts which did not go unnoticed by Matt, watching with a disapproving frown.

"The Jen-girl sure is pretty, huh?" Sean said.

Matt gave him scornful look.

"Don't get all huffy now," Sean said, and laughed at his friend's expression. "I know you're sweet on the Jen-girl." He playfully pushed Matt. "I think she digs you too." He tried, unsuccessfully, to look serious, aware of Matt's awkwardness around the girl. Sean, of course was much more mature—he thought so, anyway.

"Cut it out, man." Matt's reply was curt, showing his annoyance with Sean's game.

The mere idea that Jenny was sweet on him would have normally caused that funny feeling he always seemed to get when she tossed her hair or did that unique laugh.

But not today.

His brain felt as if it was going into overload from the events of the last few days. It had even occurred to him that maybe he was losing his mind. He had read about things like that. As he kept thinking about his experiences at the jail, he began to doubt his sanity. But he knew what he had seen and heard!

He just didn't know why or what it was. He had hoped that someone at the jail would come clean and confess the sick prank being pulled on him. He had even played detective while talking to the other employees, trying to sleuth out the culprit.

Now he was convinced that it wasn't a joke. The remaining question was: What is going on? Was he the only one who saw those things? Probably not. After all, there were all those stories about the place. He simply didn't know what to do. He knew he really needed to talk to someone, but was afraid. Like Honeyman had said when telling them about the Indian mound, "Folks might want to carry you away."

Matt glanced at Sean out of the corner of his eye, doodling in the sand. They had shared a lot of things these past few years. Though they only saw each other in the summer and were from two different worlds, they had bonded almost immediately that first summer and had grown more close each year. Probably best friends.

Sean stopped his sand scratching and asked, "What's wrong with you, man? You act like you're worried about a big exam or something," he added with a tone of concern.

Matt made his decision. "What do you think about all that stuff?" he said without looking at his friend.

"I told you. I think she's hot for you. Matter of fact, I—"

"Not that, dork!" Matt said. "The stuff Samuel and Honeyman told us." He looked at Sean. "You believe that stuff?"

"And Grandma," Sean mumbled, catching himself. "But she made me promise not to tell." He slapped the sand with his doodle stick, as if he wanted to say more.

"You mean ghost stuff?" Matt said, perking up.

"I told you, I can't say."

Matt stared at him a moment, then asked, "Well, what do you say?"

"About what? I told you I couldn't tell."

"No, I mean do you, you know, think there are ghosts?"

Sean stopped tapping the stick. "Well, I don't think Samuel or Honeyman, or Grandma would lie. I mean, a story is one thing, but they all said it was the truth, so I believe them."

"But do *you* believe there are ghosts?" Matt persisted.

Sean hit the ground with his stick. "Why you asking all that stuff, man!" he said, agitated.

"You do believe there are!"

"I didn't say that. It's just that, well ..." his voice trailed off. "I might ah saw something." His voice was barely audible.

"What," Matt said. "What did you say?"

"I said I maybe saw something!"

The two boys stared at each other.

"I did, too," Matt said in a relieved voice.

"What! You saw a ghost?" Sean exclaimed with a similar degree of relief.

"Who saw a ghost?" Jenny had returned from her shell gathering, unnoticed by the two teenagers.

"We're talking," Matt snapped, hoping Jenny would take the hint and leave.

"Well, 'scuse me," she said defiantly, using her favorite expression of late. "Since when did we stop sharing things?"

Matt melted. He looked at Sean, who shrugged.

"Between us," Matt said.

In a child-like voice she said, "Of course. Now, who saw a ghost, and were you scared."

"You know what, if you're gonna be a twit, you can just go on with your shell crap," Matt retorted in an unusually gruff manner.

"Why Matt, I've never seen that side of you. I don't think I like it."

She was trying to lighten things up, but could see Matt did not take the bait. The budding psychologist saw he was serious, and she had employed the wrong tactic.

"Oh Matt, I'm sorry. That was dumb. I'm so sorry," she added, trying to remedy her error.

Matt calmed a little. "It's OK. I just—"

"Besides," Jenny said, "there is a ton of evidence documenting a lot of really strange happenings that can't be totally explained."

"Oh, pleeease," Sean moaned. "Can you get off that psychology crap!"

"Well, you two are such wonderful conversationalists." She put her hands on her hips. "So, who saw the ghost?" she added, refusing to give up.

A lengthy silence followed.

"Are you gonna quit being a dork?" Sean demanded.

"Well, I didn't think I ..." she appraised their stares and stopped. "Yes. Now tell me." Course correction.

"I think I did," Matt said, expecting another academic response from Jenny. But it was Sean who spoke first.

"You too. No crap?"

"Yeah, at the jail. Twice."

"I saw stuff at that cemetery. So did that tourist couple," Sean said, glancing at Jenny with a warning look.

"What did you see?" Matt said, eager for details.

Totally oblivious to how it might sound, driven by the need to share his experience, Sean recounted the Tolomato events.

"What about you?" he asked Matt when he finished his story, out of breath.

The floodgates opened and Matt shared his haunting encounters.

There was a long relieved silence.

Jenny sat down cross-legged, facing the two boys. "Let me get this straight," she said. "Both of you saw ghosts, and saw stuff moving, at two places, on the same days?"

Neither boy spoke.

Jenny looked from one to the other, her eyes coming to rest on Matt. "Look, you both just started work at those old places, and there are all kinds of stories about them, even ghost tours, maybe what we have here is imagination at work."

"Oh, jeez! I knew we shouldn't have told her," Sean said, disgusted.

"Wait a sec." Jenny held a hand up. "I didn't say I didn't believe you. Besides, perception is a really weird thing. We take in stuff from our environment and it all mixes around and sometimes events trigger sensations, seeming very real, that maybe aren't what we think they are."

"You know what, if you utter one more psychology concept, Dr. Freud, I'm gonna crack you with this stick." Sean shook the stick.

"Besides," Matt chimed in, "Honeyman, Samuel and Mrs. Kirk saw some too." He glanced at Sean. "But don't say nothing 'bout Mrs. Kirk," he added, remembering Sean's promise.

"I believe you." Jenny touched Matt on the arm gently.

The goose bumps again.

"Whadda you mean, you believe me?" he managed to say over the warmth creeping up his arm from where her hand still rested.

"I believe you both saw what you believe were ghosts."

"But you don't believe they were ghosts," Sean spat out.

"Well, I wasn't there so I don't know what it was," Jenny replied in the same tone of voice as his. She also made a mental note to go to the library tomorrow and do a little research.

Neither boy spoke.

"What are you gonna do?" Jenny asked quietly.

"Will you come to the jail after work tomorrow and go through with me when I make my checks? See if you see or hear anything?" Matt looked at Sean, almost afraid to hear his answer.

"Yes. I was thinking the same thing. Right after work," Sean replied without hesitation.

Jenny stretched and looked at her two friends. She knew they were serious about this and maybe a little frightened. This was all so unlike Matt, usually so level-headed. "Well, I want to go too, but I can't, gotta go to Jacksonville with my mom again."

"You don't think there's anything to it anyway, so why would you want to go?" Matt said indignantly.

Jenny took Matt's hand and spoke softly: "Matt, I'm your friend. Your special friend, I hope. I believe you. Just please be careful."

"I, ah, I ..."

"You guys want me to leave," Sean piped in, bailing his friend out.

Jenny pushed Sean playfully and extended her hand out to Matt. "How 'bout a hand up?"

Matt jumped to the task.

CHAPTER 14

"Say Heidi, mind if I borrow Matt for a few minutes to help me move one of those tables out back?" Dave, one of the tour guides, entered the gift shop. He was dressed in a sheriff's outfit.

"Sure, Dave. Near time for him to start his jail checks, anyway. OK with you, Matt?"

"Yeah, sure." Matt had met Dave before and really enjoyed talking to him. Besides, he was hoping to kill time until Sean arrived so he could start the check with him.

"Last group cleared out a while ago, so jail's all yours when we're done," Dave said as they headed out back. "But don't let ol' Mary get you, though," he added with a laugh.

"Who's Mary?"

"Oh, nobody told you?" Dave took his Stetson off and wiped the inside with a handkerchief. "Man, it'll be dark soon and it's still hot as blazes."

He planted the hat just so on his balding head, looked at Matt and edged closer, as if to share a secret. "Well, you know that ol' place is full of spooks. People always hearing stuff." He glanced around. "'Specially like an old woman making little noises, giggling, humming, stuff such as that."

"Giggling?"

"Yeah, been reports from tourists and folks worked here for years now, that they hear something like an old woman gigglin'. Some of us figure it's ol' Mary."

"Who's old Mary, then?"

"Well, sounds like she was a turn-of-the-century version of a homeless woman. Stayed in town, no home far as anybody can tell, and a little bit coo-coo."

"Coo-coo?" Matt asked, puzzled.

"Yeah, you know, coo-coo." Dave made a circular motion with a finger by the side of his head. "Sounds harmless, though. Was in and out of jail. Very unusual to have women in jail them days. You saw that little cell, huh?"

"Yes, sir."

"Well, anyway, Mary apparently never did nu-thin' serious—petty stuff. Probably just tryin' to get by. Anyway, they was forever lockin' her up and word was, she would do stuff on purpose when she needed a place to stay. Like she lived here."

He shook his head. "Don't see why, though, that little cell right by the window. Hot in the summer, cold in the winter, and wet for days when it rained." He laughed. "No accountin' for taste in comfort, huh? Anyway, Mary died in the jail when she was pretty old, so we figure she still lives here 'cause she likes it and got nowhere else to go, and she gigglin' 'cause she got the whole place now." Dave eyed Matt. "You ain't heard her, huh?"

Matt thought a moment. "Well, you know, that old place, echoes and all."

"Well, you might run into ol' Mary, you being the only one in there when you make your rounds." He wiped his brow again. "You know, there's been ghost hunters and such roam through this place. Trying to get to the bottom of all those stories people been tellin'. I was told they never left disap-pointed, and they talked to folks that saw or heard stuff, and a lot of those stories were very similar." He eyeballed Matt. "You didn't see nuthin' yet, huh?"

Dave laughed before Matt could answer. "Come on, let's move this thing over by that tree. Got a group gonna eat out here tomorrow."

That job finished, Matt headed back around the building.

Heidi waved as she headed to her car. "See you tomorrow, Matt. Don't forget to lock up."

"OK, Heidi."

Matt looked around anxiously for Sean and decided to go ahead and pick up trash around the gallows area when he didn't see him.

He thought about Dave's story while walking around the south end of the jail, his head down, contemplating the giggles he had in fact heard.

He gasped and jumped when he turned the corner and almost bumped into Sean.

Matt exclaimed, "Crap, man, what are you doing!"

Sean countered in bravado fashion, "Well, whadda you think I'm doing, doofus. We're gonna find them spooks, remember?"

"Yeah, I remember. Come on, help me pick up this trash first."

"OK," Matt asked as he scooped up the last piece of trash, "you sure you want to do this?"

"Absolutely. We need to figure this out. I'm ready. Let's do it," Sean responded. "Besides," he added, "it doesn't seem like they want to hurt us." He thought a moment. "'Cept maybe that one at the graveyard."

"Yeah, let's go," Matt said. He opened the rear door and entered.

The circuit through the downstairs cell areas and kitchen complete, they approached the sheriff's office.

Matt stopped. "This is the first place I heard stuff."

"You want me to go first?" Sean asked, still sounding braver than he felt.

"No, that's OK," Matt said. "Let's go together."

The boys entered the office and stood silently for a moment, then proceeded back to the parlor.

When nothing happened, Matt was both relieved and disappointed.

"Let's go upstairs," he said, concerned that Sean might not believe his story since it was now quiet.

"Everything OK here?" Sean asked.

"Whadda you mean? You hear something?"

"No, but you do get paid to check stuff, don't you? So, did you check?"

"Oh. Yeah." Matt glanced around and adjusted a small table picture someone had knocked over.

"OK. Let's go up."

As the boys reached the stairway's top landing, Jenny was entering the back door. Having returned from Jacksonville early, she had decided she needed to be a part of this event. She followed the same path they had taken on the previous tour, heading toward the sheriff's office, where she expected to find the boys.

Matt and Sean approached the upstairs bedroom door as it slowly opened, causing them to stop abruptly.

They retreated a step, and the door partially closed with a moan.

They exchanged glances, seeking reassurance, and stepped forward again. The door opened wider, as if inviting them in. The sound of creaking hinges was mixed with a low giggle from within the room.

Matt whispered, "You hear that?"

"Yeah. Sounds like an old woman."

"Ahhhhh. Three scared little boys," a voice said, followed by a "tsh, tsh" sound.

"Who are you?" Sean asked.

"Who are you?" the voice repeated.

"You're Mary, aren't you?" Matt asked, recalling Dave's story.

"Ahhhhhhh. Smart little boy," Mary said, then started humming, the sound coming from various parts of the room, as if she were walking around.

"Who's the other boy? There's only two of us. You said three," Sean asked.

"Maybe with your little girly friend," she said, lapsing into uncontrollable giggles. The quilt rose up from the bed like a magic carpet and starting waving as if being shaken.

The boys retreated backward again.

"Matt!"

"That's Jenny!" Matt yelled. "Downstairs."

They bolted to the stairwell and clamored down the stairs, sprinting to the office as Jenny emerged, shaken. She grabbed Matt's hand.

Nearly breathless, she whispered, "I saw something."

Matt said, "Wh-what are y-you doing here? Wh-what d-did you see?"

She squeezed his hand tighter. "I don't know. I, I ..."

"Just catch your breath. You're OK," Matt reassured her.

Jenny took a deep breath and calmed herself. When she was able to speak in a normal voice she said, "I saw a shape. It was in the parlor and came toward me."

The boys looked through the office toward the parlor.

Sean walked across the office floor cautiously and peeked around the corner of the center fireplace.

"There's nothing here," he reported.

"Well, it was here!" Jenny said defensively.

"What was it, exactly. What did you see?" Matt said, encouraging her.

She thought a moment. "OK. It was a shape, smaller than us, kind of bluish-white and it kinda flowed. Wavy-like." She looked toward the parlor, replaying the scene in her mind. "And as it came toward me, it kinda changed shape, like you were molding clay into a figure."

"Was the shape maybe like a young boy?" Matt asked.

"Yes. Maybe. I don't know," she replied, exasperated.

"What did it do? Did it speak?" Sean had returned to the office area.

"Yes. Yes. It did!" she exclaimed. "In a kind of garbled voice." She shook her head. "It said, 'Can you help me?' and when it spoke, its form grew even more clear."

"Did you answer? What did you do?" Sean asked.

"I didn't do anything. ... I don't think I was actually afraid, but I just couldn't think. It's so strange."

"Well, why did you scream like that? Sounded to me like you were scared," Sean questioned in a concerned tone.

"No, I yelled because when it got about five or six feet from me, something slammed into that window," she said, and pointed to the side office window. "And I guess I freaked."

"What next?" Sean had become head interrogator.

"It disappeared."

"Whadda you mean, it disappeared?" he demanded.

"I mean it disappeared. When whatever it was hit the window, it seemed to shake, real weird-like, and just disappeared. Like it scared him too."

"You said him. So was it a boy or not?" Sean persisted.

"It was hard to tell. I think it was, but I'm not sure."

The boys exchanged looks.

"Well, who made you the inquisitor, anyway? I'm not sure what it was." Her eyes misted over, as if she were on the verge of tears.

"No, Jen-girl, I didn't mean anything. I'm trying to figure this thing out," Sean said, hoping to reassure her.

"Yeah, Jen, we saw some strange stuff upstairs." Matt snapped his fingers. "Wait a minute, Mary, or whoever up there said a boy was with our friend."

They were quiet, contemplating Matt's revelation.

Jenny shivered. "It's cold in here."

The silence of the old room was like the inside of a vault. Absolutely no noise. Not even from outside.

Matt said, "Yeah, it is col—"

The desk chair had begun shaking. Faster and faster it shook, banging the floor, the noise echoing through the ancient building.

Without speaking they turned and ran for the door, Jenny still clutching Matt's hand in a death grip. They didn't slow down until they were standing near The Beast and Jenny's moped.

"Let's get outta here. We need to figure this out," Sean said.

"Can I have my hand, now?" Matt said to Jenny, not really wanting to let go, but needing relief from the pain of her tight grip.

"Oh," she said with a nervous laugh. "I'm sorry."

"It's OK. I'm not," Matt said soothingly, surprised at his own boldness.

"Well, tell you what. Since there ain't many people around to see me, why don't I drive the flamingo and Jenny can ride with you," Sean said.

"Good idea," Matt quickly said. "OK with you?" he added, looking at Jenny with anxiety.

"Yeah. That's a good idea." She sounded relieved. "Oh, when we get back, you guys go to my gazebo out back and I'll meet you there. I have to get something from the house first."

"OK, let's go," Matt said quickly, excited over the prospect of riding Jenny on The Beast, hoping of course that he would be in top form for the trip.

CHAPTER 15

Matt and Sean sat in Jenny's gazebo as instructed while she retrieved something from her house.

"So, you need more proof Jenny's sweet on you, dork?" Sean said in a tone of great wisdom.

"What's that 'sposed to mean?"

"Well, who did she yell for when she got scared?"

"Aw, that's just because we've known each other so long." Matt felt embarrassed and in no mood to be joshed.

"Yeah, and that's why she held your hand the whole time," Sean countered. "Can you understand the words comin' outta my lips?" he added, using the expression from a recent popular movie.

"You're making a big deal outta nothing."

"Man, you gotta get your confidence level up. Can you feel me, man?" Now on a roll, Sean began a melodramatic embellishment of the situation. "I'm telling you—"

"OK. I had to get my notebook."

Mercifully, Jenny returned, cutting Sean off.

"I thought it might help if we understood a little more about what we're dealing with, so I did a little research."

"Well, looks to me like we're dealing with ghosts," Sean cut in. "I don't see why we need any more of your psychology lectures."

Matt said, "Wait a minute, Sean. It might not hurt to understand more about what's going on." He turned his attention to Jenny.

She said, "That's right, Yankee boy. For instance, you said we're dealing with ghosts. Well, that term means someone or something that exists without a body, yet can be perceived by those of us living. Parapsychologists who study this stuff say there are actually at least three categories of 'ghosts': apparitions, haunting and poltergeists."

"Well, they're all ghosts, aren't they?" Sean cut in.

"But there are differences. That's the whole point. And they do different things."

"Well, they're dead and they're still hanging around, that's all I need to know." Sean was not convinced her lecture was necessary.

"So what's the difference?" Matt chimed in.

Sean moaned.

"OK. Hauntings are usually connected to locations, you know, like a building, land, even an object, like furniture. Some parapsychologists say that somehow the environment picks up information from people and events and records it, then people sometimes can pick up pieces of the recordings. At least that's kinda the scientific explanation. I guess not all of 'em go along with it."

"And what about apparitions?" Matt asked.

"They are consciousness without a body and can be seen, heard, felt, smelled and can somehow exist after the death of the body. They can actually have personality or intelligence." Jenny paused, studying her notes. "An apparition," she continued, "can interact with the living and each other—that's what separates them from haunting ghosts. I think that's what we saw tonight." She looked at the boys for a response.

"Well, what about those leaves swirling and wind blowing and all that stuff?" Sean asked.

"Ahhh. Next category. Poltergeist, which literally means 'noisy ghost.' Now with these cases, physical effects are the theme. Things like movements, levitation, appearance and disappearance of objects, unexplained behavior of electrical things, like lights going on and off and so on."

Sean thought about the cemetery light. "So they're the bad dudes," he said.

"Not necessarily, but they are very active. Sometimes act like they're upset or mad. Throw stuff." She paused. "And I guess some are bad dudes."

"That's something," Matt said.

"So you don't think these guys mean us any harm?" Sean asked.

"Well, there's no way I can know that. I'm not an expert. Actually, I don't know if anybody really is. It is unexplained phenomena, you know," she said with decision.

"Well, that's a big help," Sean said, stretching.

"Look, whatever or whoever I saw tonight asked me if I could help it, or him, or whatever. I don't think that was meant to harm," Jenny retorted.

"Well, what about the window thing, and the flying stick I saw?" Sean countered.

"I don't know," Jenny said thoughtfully.

"We need to talk to someone who knows about this stuff. I mean—" he caught himself, not wanting to hurt Jenny's feelings.

"I agree. I'm only telling you what I read. I don't know any more than you guys," Jenny said, quickly letting Matt know she understood his statement.

"Well, I guess I agree, too. But who? Whoever it is will probably think we're crazy," Sean said.

"What about that woman Samuel mentioned? You know, Hattie, I think it was," Matt said.

"Oh shoot, man. Ray at the drugstore mentioned her. Sounds like some palm reader witch tryin' to make a buck," Sean said, not convinced.

"I don't know. Samuel seemed to think highly of her," Matt threw back.

"I guess." Sean shrugged.

"Are you talking about Hattie over in Lincolnville?" Jenny asked.

"I don't know where she lives. Why?" Matt said.

"My friend Marcy told me about her one time. Some folks had her chase away evil spirits and such. I don't think she's a witch, though." She shot a disapproving look at Sean.

The three teens sat for a few moments, thinking.

Breaking the silence, Jenny said decisively, "Well, we need to do something. I say we go see Samuel tomorrow. Find out what he thinks about seeing the Hattie woman."

"I agree," Matt said.

They looked at Sean.

"Hey, I know when I'm outvoted. Let's do it."

"OK. Come to my house at eight in the morning. I'll make pancakes and then we'll go see Samuel," Jenny said.

"Eight o'clock in the morning! A.M.!" Sean exclaimed.

"Yeah, that's good. We can catch Samuel at the stable right after, before he leaves for his carriage rides," Matt said, ignoring Sean's outburst.

"OK. See you tomorrow."

Jenny strode away, with a lingering backward glance at Matt, an act which did not go unnoticed by Sean.

When Jenny disappeared into her house, Sean said, "So, should I be late in the morning to give you and Jenny time to mooneye and such?"

"You don't quit, do you, dork?" Matt responded. "Actually, I was kinda thinking about asking her about maybe going to all the July Fourth stuff. But I can't seem to find the right time."

"Hey man, you didn't see that look she just gave you? Make a move, dude. The girl's waitin'. *Just* do it! I'm telling you."

"Yeah. I don't know."

"Oh man, I'm going to bed. You make me tired," Sean said as he stood up. He started to walk away, then turned back. He said to Matt, "Just ... do ... it. Sean, the sage personally guarantees you will like the results. See you tomorrow."

"Yeah, OK," Matt said. "Sean," he added.

"Yeah." Sean turned.

"Thanks, man."

"Hey, what are buddies for? Later."

CHAPTER 16

"Hey, Samuel," Matt called out as the three kids approached the stables located downtown on a small side street.

Samuel stopped brushing Blackout and turned. "Well, what you boys and girls doin' out so early this fine morning?"

"Oh, just messin' around."

"Just messin' 'round, huh?" Samuel gave his visitors an inquisitive look. "Well, here, mess 'round with this ol' goat while I get his harness." He handed Matt the brush. "You remember how?"

"Sure I do," Matt retorted with injured pride.

Samuel lifted the harness from its rail and put it smoothly on the horse.

"Hand them straps under to me, Sean," Samuel directed. He grabbed the worn leather being pushed under Blackout's belly and began buckling them down.

Matt brushed Blackout gently as the three youngsters exchanged glances.

"Say, Samuel, that lady you told us about," Matt started.

"What lady?"

"You know, the one you talked about. Hattie."

"Miss Hattie," Samuel corrected.

"Yeah, Miss Hattie. Well, we was wondering if we could talk to her?"

"Whataya wanna talk to Miss Hattie fo'?" Samuel kept working on the straps. "She kinda keep to herself, you know. Gettin' old."

"Well, we wanted to ask her some things, 'bout spirits and all."

"What fo'? You been seein' some?" Samuel fussed at the horse for expanding his belly so the cinch wouldn't be so tight once he relaxed.

Samuel looked at Matt when there was no response. He could tell they were all anxious.

"Probably wouldn't take long," Matt finally said. "I heard she lives somewhere around here."

"Yeah. You right. Right behind these stables, one street over. She don't much cottin' to company, though." Samuel was not convinced it was a good idea.

"It's really important, Samuel." Jenny entered the exchange. "And I promise I won't let these guys get carried away," she said.

Samuel raised from his chore and ran his tongue over his thin lips. His leathery face wrinkled into a grin. "Now, I 'spect you could keep these two scoundrels under control all right." He looked thoughtful for a moment.

"Tell you what," he finally said, "I don't know what you kids up to, but I guess you got your reasons. Ol' Blackout needs to finish his breakfast, so I'll walk you over to Miss Hattie's. If she favors your visit, I'll come on back, but if'n she busy, then we all jus' come on back. How'd that be?" he asked.

"That's great! Can we go now?" Matt urged, relieved.

"May as well. This ol' goat gone take all day to eat. Come on."

CHAPTER 17

July 1, A.M.

Miss Hattie's house yelled her name as soon as they rounded the corner. Very small, cypress lapboard construction and old. A tiny porch, barely able to accommodate three faded green rockers, was home to a large variety of plants and shells. A long string of garlic cloves guarded the front stoop.

Sean whispered to Matt, "Maybe she really is a witch."

"Now, if you boys gone act like fools, we'll go on back," Samuel said.

"Sean!" Jenny scolded.

"OK. OK. I was kidding. Sorry."

Samuel stopped and waggled his finger at the boys. "Now, Miss Hattie a little strange, but she a good woman. Helps lots of folks." He eyeballed Sean. "You jus' remember that."

"Yes sir," Sean responded, embarrassed.

Samuel held his gaze a moment, then turned and knocked on the cypress screen door.

"What you want?" a voice yelled out.

"It's Samuel, Miss Hattie."

They could hear footsteps shuffling across a bare floor.

"Ain't saw you in a month of Sundays."

A small, withered, old woman opened the door. Snow-white hair highlighted a frail but somehow sinewy-appearing body so wrinkled that her features were difficult to distinguish.

"Yes ma'am, Miss Hattie, and I need to come pay you a visit and sit 'n' rock." Samuel shuffled slightly, trying to be respectful. "But today, I got me some tourists to haul." He nodded toward the three youngsters. "This here is Matt, Jenny and Sean. They's pretty good kids and they wanted to speak with you if you was of a mind to."

"What you reckon they want?" She directed her comment at Samuel with not even a glance at the other three.

127

"Well, Miss Hattie, I jus' think I might let them tell you that," Samuel replied, adding, "if you ain't too busy."

The old woman's eyes looked the three astonished teens over, coming to rest on Sean.

"You there, boy, where you from? You ain't from 'round here," she demanded accusingly.

"Ah, New York, ma'am. Ah, New York City," Sean stammered, caught off guard.

She repeated slowly, "New York City." Then asked, "Whatcha doin' way down here with all these dumb ol' rednecks?"

"Well, I, ah, I'm visiting my friend Matt. He lives here." Sean started to sweat. "And my grandmother. I've been coming every summer." He hoped that would compensate for the fact that Miss Hattie didn't seem to care much for out-o'-towners.

"Why you keep comin' back?" The woman was not through with the interrogation.

Sean looked first to Matt, then Samuel for help, but none was forthcoming.

"Well, I don—I hadn't thought about it. I guess because I like it here. It's a neat place." Struggling, Sean said, "It just sort of gets in you."

There was the slightest hint of a twinkle in the old woman's eyes. Her voice softened slightly.

"Well, guess it do at that." She turned from the group and went inside.

Samuel shrugged when the kids looked to him for guidance.

"Go on to your tourists, Samuel. Come back and sit with me when you can. You kids come in here. Wipe your feet," Miss Hattie directed them from inside the house.

"Yes ma'am, Miss Hattie. I'll sure do that. You send these boys and girls on outta here when you get tired of 'em," Samuel answered for the group. When there was no response, he gestured toward the door and headed down the steps.

The three teens huddled in the center of the front room and watched Miss Hattie drop into a well-worn rocker-recliner. A couch was nearby, but she did not extend an offer for its use to the kids.

No one spoke as she settled in and started rocking.

After a while she said, "Ya'll gone stand there all day or you gone tell me what you want?"

Matt swallowed hard. "Well, I work over at the Old Jail on San Marco—"

"I know where it is, boy. What you think, ol' Hattie dumb or sumptin'?"

129

"No, ma'am. I didn't mean ... I mean ... well, anyway, I been seeing stuff over there."

The old woman rocked silently.

"Boy, you gone tell me what's on your mind or not?" Hattie asked when Matt did not continue.

He blurted out, "I saw some ghosts!"

"Apparitions," Jenny corrected.

The woman glanced at Jenny. "Everybody sees ghosts 'roun here," she said matter-of-factly. She closed her eyes and kept rocking.

The kids looked at each other, unsure if Hattie was still awake.

"What else?" Hattie spoke, eyes still shut.

Jenny elbowed Matt.

"But I seen 'em more than once. A woman named Mary—"

Hattie's eyes popped opened, causing Matt to stop in mid-sentence. She kept rocking.

"Act kinda strange," she stated, rather than asked.

"Yes ma'am, she giggles a lot."

"That's ol' crazy Mary. She one of them decided to stay in between. She ain't gone hurt you."

Confused at the old woman's calm demeanor and casual acceptance of their sightings, Jenny said, "But I saw, uh, maybe a little boy. He asked me to help him."

"Nuttin' but another soul caught in between," Hattie repeated.

"What do you mean, in between?" Jenny had already read about this but was curious if Hattie was referring to the same thing.

"In between. When some folks die, they don't go up, they don't go down. They just stay in between. Spirits."

"Why?" Jenny persisted.

The old woman glanced at her briefly and shut her eyes again. "Well now, that's kinda hard to say. Some spirits want to stay, least for a while. Probably Mary. She pretty much lived at that jail. Then some others can't go, or won't go, for some reason or other. All kind of reasons. Hard to say. Maybe why that boy ask you to help." She yawned and continued rocking, eyes shut.

"How come they only heard Mary and couldn't see her, and I could see the boy, or at least something?" Jenny asked, entering her research mode.

"Spirit decides. Sometime they show, sometime not," Hattie stated simply. "What you think, missy?" she added with slight interest in her tone.

Picking up the cue, Jenny replied, "Well, maybe the more they want to be with you, or if they need your help, or are trying to tell you something, the more they'll show themselves. Or maybe they're just curious."

"You don't need ol' Hattie. You kin figure this out," she said with an ever so slight hint of a smile.

"But Sean saw another boy at the cemetery," Jenny said.

"Mor'n one spirit, missy. Might be the same one movin' 'round." She kept rocking, eyes closed. "What cemetery?" she asked.

"By the drugstore. Tolomato," Sean replied.

Her eyes popped open and she scolded Sean. "You best stay 'way from that place. There's evil there. You hear me now."

"But something threw a limb at the spirit, the boy, and stuff was flying around—"

Interrupting, Matt said, "Yeah, and something hit the window at the jail and scared that spirit away."

She stopped rocking again. "Smell something?" She looked at Sean.

"It was awful." He made a face as he recalled the stench.

Jenny could stay quiet no longer. "Was it a poltergeist?"

"Uneasy spirits. Restless. Get upset easy and knock things 'round." She looked from one to the other and shook her head. Her eyes saddened as she spoke. "Ain't good that boy in that ol' place with one of them unhappy spirits."

"He told me to be careful and to run," Sean said. "That's when the limb hit him."

She shook her white head. "Um, um, um. That po' soul. He probably scared and cain't or won't leave. That po' boy." She sighed. "Ain't nothing to be done." She sighed again, as if the sadness tired her.

She spoke sharply to Sean. "You best stay 'way from that place. You hear me?" she asked, a concerned tone in her wavering voice.

"But can't we help them?" Jenny pleaded.

"Missy, this ain't nuttin' you can fix 'cause you don't know what keepin' them in between. Probably nuttin' to be done even if you did know. Them spirits won't hurt you." She looked at Sean again. "Just you stay back from that graveyard. There's evil spirits there. Call 'em what you want," she said, looking at Jenny. "Can sense things. They can trick you. You stay 'way. You hear me now."

"Yes ma'am."

"You all go on now. Miss Hattie needs a nap," she said, curtly dismissing the kids.

The teens looked at each other but didn't move.

"You kids deaf, too? Go on. And leave them spirits to their own world. Ain't none of your concern."

The trio left reluctantly, not sure what they accomplished or, more important, what their next step would be.

CHAPTER 18

Hattie was exhausted from the exchange and, she had to confess to herself, saddened by the revelation of what was obviously a trapped little boy, maybe two, in that frightening world that is the "in between."

Her meeting with the kids weighed heavily on her mind for hours, until finally she dozed.

She awoke sometime later with a start.

Her mind was fuzzy from sleep as she struggled to rise from the rocker. Never concerned with clocks and such, she moved to the window and looked out.

Late afternoon, she thought.

As she made her way to the small kitchen to prepare a cup of her special tea, her thoughts began to get more organized and she reflected on her meeting with the youngsters.

Suddenly she was overwhelmed with sadness as she thought of the little boy in that place with a restless spirit.

"Why don't that child go on?" she mumbled to herself.

She grunted, dropped the tea bag and headed to the closet for her hat. She went out the back door tugging the hat on, and rolled her three-wheel bike out of its tiny shed.

Her face fixed in grim determination, she started up Riberia Street toward Tolomato Cemetery, unsure what she might accomplish, but hopeful she could discover something that might reveal what was behind the sightings the kids had witnessed.

Relieved, she finally found herself on the last stretch of street leading to the cemetery. Though fatigued, she felt curiously alive. It was near dusk. Most workers and day tourists had cleared out, and night strollers were still enjoying dinner or drinks before their outings.

With great coolness and deliberation, she moved closer to Tolomato. As she did so, she became conscious that she was thinking about scenes that were unfamiliar to her. She seemed to be recalling scenes from another person's memory. A tall ship, its majestic sails full in the wind sliding past the old fort, and something, yes, a smaller boat, young voices crying out.

Probably, she reckoned, she was thinking the thoughts of another person, from another time. She knew of this phenomena, for she was no stranger to spirits.

With not a little trepidation, she found herself on the walkway in front of the cemetery.

She stopped the bike and glimpsed a faint glow toward the rear of the graveyard. She knew it was not a light since it moved toward her and began to take on a form.

"Come on, boy, to ol' Hattie," she said from the bike, seeking to coax the child, if it was a child, nearer to her so she could get it to speak.

The form moved closer, its shape more defined.

She began to dismount from her bike so she could move to the fence, but found she could not move. Something was holding her.

Struggle as she might, she could not get off the bike.

The form was stationary, no longer moving toward her.

It moved farther away as debris from the cemetery pelted Hattie. Her bike started shaking, the loose fenders making a loud clattering sound as they banged against the frame.

"You done jumped on ol' Hattie now," she said aloud, determination overcoming fear.

Her hat flew off and a mass in the swirling leaves popped and cracked. An image of a thousand electrical arcs outlined the shape of something unrecognizable.

She struggled to free her hands from the handlebars, yelling out, "You ain't scarin' ol' Hattie. I done seen your kind before!"

The bike rose off the ground, the wheels spinning wildly, fenders clanging. The light impulses danced more furiously, now accompanied by a deep snarling sound.

As quickly as it had begun, the noise and light show stopped, and the bike crashed to the ground, spilling the now freed Hattie.

A car screeched to a halt and a man ran toward Hattie while his wife peered from the car window, her hand clasped over her mouth in disbelief.

"Lady, are you all right?" He helped Hattie to her feet. "Your bike looked like it was about to take off!" the man said without pause. "And what the hell was that in the graveyard? I never seen nothing like this." The man was flabbergasted.

"I'm fine, boy," Hattie said, patting the man's hand gently. "I got to get this old bike worked on. Thing wants to take off sometime." She laughed. "Ain't nuttin' to worry 'bout. You go on now 'fore somebody run over your car. Thank you kindly for your help."

"Oh, jeez!" The man hurried to his idling vehicle.

Hattie turned back to the cemetery but knew nothing would be there. "That evil thing controlling that child," she said aloud. "I ain't through you. Ol' Hattie gone see you again."

Disappointed, she maneuvered the bike around and headed back home.

Suddenly she stopped.

Mary.

Maybe she could connect with Mary, or whoever it was at the jail. Find out something.

"I need to see that boy," she said, and began pedaling faster, covering the short street blocks in the light traffic with all the speed she could muster.

Rolling into the stable driveway, Hattie said, "Samuel ... I need ... to see that boy ... what's his name ... at the jail."

"Hattie, what the dickens you doin' out here? Can't you see it nearly dark?" Samuel managed to reply in spite of his astonishment. Blackout moved restlessly, waiting to be unhitched and fed.

Hattie dismounted from her bike. "Is that boy ... over at the jail?"

"What boy? What you talkin' 'bout?"

"That boy you brought to my house," she said impatiently. "Matt," she added, remembering his name, "he at that jail right now?"

"Well, yeah, Miss Hattie, I reckon he is, but he ..." His voice trailed off as he watched Hattie stomp to his truck.

"Come on, take me there."

Samuel looked at the woman and knew it would be useless to argue. He scooped a handful of oats and put them in Blackout's feedbag.

"OK, Miss Hattie, come on," he said, shaking his head in resignation.

CHAPTER 19

Matt completed his jail check almost without incident—thanks, he suspected, to the presence of two talkative electricians completing a new cable installation. One, from his position upstairs, yelled directions to the other located downstairs throughout Matt's rounds. He heard low giggles both upstairs and down, as if he were being followed, but nothing else.

Mr. Usina had told him to stay until the workmen finished and left. Now, as darkness fell, they were finally driving out of the empty parking lot. Matt locked up and headed to The Beast when Samuel's truck drove into the lot.

Surprised, Matt approached the vehicle and could see Samuel sitting behind the wheel.

"Samuel, what are you do—"

Stepping from the passenger compartment, Hattie cut him off. "Come on, boy, I need to go in that jail." She came around the truck.

Matt looked at Samuel for an explanation.

"Can you take her in? She ain't gone leave till you do."

"What's going on?" Matt asked.

"Don' know. She showed up at the stable and here we are. Wouldn't talk all the way over here. Leastways to me. Kept mumbling to herself." He shook his head. "I hope she's all right. You may as well take her in 'cause she ain't leavin' till you do." He was watching Hattie walk toward the jail. "You gone hafta get her back, too. I got ol' Blackout standing in his harness yet."

"OK. I'll take care of her," Matt said, sensing Samuel's concern. He ran after Hattie.

"You see them spirits in there tonight?" she asked when he caught up.

"Just giggling. She followed me around giggling. I think I hurt her feelings. There were a couple of workmen in there, so maybe she's bashful."

"What 'bout that other'n? That boy?" she said, ignoring his joke.

"No. Well, I think I heard a voice once, like soft crying, but I'm not sure."

They reached the rear door. Matt unlocked and held it open for Hattie.

"Take me to where you saw 'em," she directed as she stepped in.

"OK. We'll go downstairs first, then upstairs."

"You saw 'em in both places?"

"Yeah, or heard them."

They arrived at the office and Matt started in, suddenly realizing he would probably get fired if anyone caught him in here with this old woman, though somehow that seemed unimportant right now.

"Nuttin' in here," Hattie stated from the doorway.

"Well, how do you know? Maybe they're in the parlor," Matt retorted.

"Nuttin' in here," she repeated, "come on."

Matt moved past her and headed up the stairs. He approached the bedroom and tried to enter, but like before, it was as if something was in the way.

Stepping back, he whispered, "Something's there."

"I know," Hattie said, stepping closer and putting her hand out.

She touched something solid but soft, like a person.

"You scared to let us in, spirit?" Hattie challenged.

They heard a series of hysterical giggles, followed by, "Come in, dearie."

"I know you, Mary. I used to see you when I was a little girl. Long time ago." Hattie spoke as if she were talking to a real person.

"Ohhhhhh," came a reply in a high, whiney voice.

The bed quilt started flapping like before.

"Why are you still here? This ol' cold place. Why don't you leave, if you can?" Hattie spoke, ignoring the quilt.

"Mary lives here. Don't hafta leave. Home," Mary responded, taking Hattie's bait to determine if she were trapped by something.

Mary was humming now.

Casually strolling around the bedroom, Hattie asked, "How 'bout that boy? You keepin' him here?"

Her question was met with silence.

"Come on, boy, this silly ol' spirit don't know nothin'." She turned as if to leave, surprising Matt.

When they reached the door, Mary said, "That John, he can leave if he want. He a scared little boy."

Hattie turned back.

"Then why won't he leave? I think you holdin' him."

"Am not," Mary responded indignantly. "He just a silly boy. Won't leave his friend."

They heard soft sobbing.

Hattie asked soothingly, "John, is that you, child?"

The sobbing continued. They could barely make out a shape in the back bedroom door ... very dim.

Mary giggled. "See, he just a scared little boy. He leaves sometime. Goes to that ol' fort, but always comes back, starts crying, like he doing now. Boo hoo hoo," she mimicked.

"Is he goin' there tonight?" Hattie asked.

"No, just sometime. Soon, maybe."

"Why does he go?" Matt surprised himself, asking a spirit a question.

"Don' know. Playin', maybe. He just silly."

"John, child, talk to ol' Hattie. Why you don't leave this place? Go rest."

The shape glowed brighter. For the first time, Matt could tell it was indeed a young boy, maybe eleven or twelve.

"My friend," a barely audible voice responded, followed by sobbing.

"John, who is your fr—" Hattie stopped in mid-sentence when the small wooden train set on the floor jerked to a start and began moving in a circle.

Pictures rattled against the walls and the train spun around faster and faster, then scattered across the floor.

The glowing shape that was John dimmed slowly and then disappeared.

A chair flew across the room, narrowly missing Hattie, and crashed to the floor. The temperature dropped and Matt could see his breath coming in rapid bursts from fright. It felt like an ice storage locker he recalled going in one time.

"Mary, who is th—" Hattie started saying, then started gagging.

Matt put his hand over his mouth as the foul stench filled his nostrils.

Hattie pushed him toward the door with one hand while she held the other tightly across her mouth. Matt grabbed her arm as she stumbled on the stairs and a glass picture flew over their heads and shattered against the rail. A sound like the thumping of a hundred feet on a floor came from the bedroom and ice cold air surrounded them.

They both began coughing and gasping for breath when Matt finally flung the outside door open.

"Hattie, you all right?" he asked.

Hattie gasped, clutching her chest. "We done here."

Matt couldn't believe how calm she was after what had just happened. She acted like it was an everyday occurrence.

"Take me home, boy," Hattie said as they approached the parking lot. "Where's your car?" she added, looking around.

Oh boy, Matt thought, this oughta be good.

"Well, I have a bike." He pointed to The Beast. "But I can call my dad to come in his Jeep," Matt offered.

The old lady walked up to the Indian.

"I seen these things aroun'. Always wanted to ride in one." She laughed like a girl and started trying to figure out how to get in the sidecar. With Matt's help she finally succeeded.

"Les' go," she ordered as she settled in.

Matt reached for his extra helmet. "You have to wear this," he said, handing it to her.

"I ain't wearin' that thing. I needs some air," she said with finality, pushing the hard shell away.

"Miss Hattie, you have to wear it. You gonna get me in trouble. I already stuck my neck taking you in the jail."

She eyed the helmet. "Give it to me." She snatched the helmet from his hand.

Matt cranked The Beast and headed down San Marco.

He turned onto Riberia and waved at Samuel and Sean as they passed the stable. He saw Sean take off in a run after them.

"Boy, I done seen everythin' now," Samuel said, watching the group disappear.

Sean came running up as Matt was helping Hattie onto her porch.

"You're a pretty good driver," the old lady said while easing into one of the rockers.

"What happened?" Sean asked, out of breath. "Samuel told me you and Miss Hattie went to the jail."

Matt told him about their encounter.

Hattie was silent throughout his discourse.

"What are we gonna do?" Sean asked.

Samuel pulled up in his truck and took the bike out of the back.

"You OK, Miss Hattie?"

The old woman did not speak. Her chair creaked as she gently rocked, her eyes closed.

"Miss Hattie," Samuel called to her softly.

"You boys go on home. Miss Hattie gots to think."

Samuel motioned the boys away.

"You boys go on home. Miss Hattie need to rest."

"But ..." Matt started.

Samuel held his hand up. "Go on, now. Tomorrow another day."

CHAPTER 20

July 2, A.M.

Matt jerked awake.

"What th—" he responded, still half asleep, to the persistent tapping on his bedroom window.

"Matt. Matt."

He glared at the window where Sean was again tapping.

With a moan, Matt moved across the room and stared out at his friend.

"What are you doin'?" He glanced back at the clock on his nightstand. "It's not even eight o'clock."

"Let me in, dude. We gotta go help my grandma."

"Why didn't you go to the door?"

"I did, dummy. No one answered. Let me in."

"Oh yeah," Matt replied, vaguely recalling his mom sticking her head in earlier to advise him she had to leave for an appointment.

"Go around." Matt staggered to the front door.

"What's wrong with Mrs. Kirk?" he asked, hoping the old lady wasn't ill.

"Nothin'. She wants us to help Mrs. Masters move a couch in her house."

"Mrs. Masters? Next door? A couch?" Matt replied, confused.

"Yes, dummy. You know, one of them things more than one person can sit on. We're gonna help her move a couch from one side of the room to the other. Get dressed."

"You got me out of bed to move a couch?" Matt stated in disbelief. "We can move a couch anytime."

"No we can't. Grandma asked me twice already, and we been so busy, I keep forgetting. Now, Grandma has to go down to Flagler with her group, and she wants to be there when we move the thing. Come on."

"So the reason I'm standing here early in the morning is because you couldn't remember something?"

"Will you get dressed? Let's get this over with."

With a shake of his head, Matt stomped off to his bedroom.

"You figured out our next move on this ghost deal?" Sean asked as they crossed the street.

"No, but I ain't crazy 'bout goin' back in the jail with that evil spirit or whatever it was." Matt shook his head.

"Yeah. I don't blame you. I wonder if it—"

"Matt, I sure hope Sean didn't wake you. He said you got up early," Mrs. Kirk said from the porch.

"No problem at all, Mrs. Kirk," he said, glancing at Sean.

"Well, let's go on over, then," she said, and turned back. "You boys be on your best behavior now. Maria is a very proper lady. Minorcan, you know. One of the oldest families in town."

She started walking, then turned again. "Oh, and say something nice about some of her old stuff. She's so proud of all those family heirlooms."

"Yes ma'am," the boys chimed in unison.

The boys entered after carefully wiping their feet per Mrs. Masters' directions, and Matt felt as though he had stepped back in time, as he always did when in her house, which wasn't often. A retired science teacher, Mrs. Masters was friendly enough, but kept to herself except for her close friend, Mrs. Kirk.

Everything in the room was old and orderly. The small table in the middle of the room had probably been moved from the now empty wall across the room.

The outer wall continuing from the door was pierced by two beautifully carved lattice-panel windows, ending into a huge built-in goody case, as his dad called them; shelf after shelf filled with antique treasures. Down from the wall corner was a fireplace, its mantel also overburdened with stuff. Next to the fireplace was the turn-of-the-century couch, or settee, which, Matt surmised, was to be moved to the empty wall.

"Now boys, if you don't mind, I want to move that settee," she said, pointing delicately, "right over there." She pointed again, verifying Matt's reconnoiter. She added, "And do be ever so careful."

"Yes ma'am," they again replied in unison.

The boys set about the chore at hand.

"Oh, that's perfect," Mrs. Masters said after the boys put the settee in place.

As Mrs. Masters reached over the couch to straighten an already straight wall picture, Sean remembered his grandma's request.

"Wow, that's a really old picture. Great frame." He looked at his grandma for approval, but saw instead a slight frown.

"Oh. Yes. Over a hundred years old." She hesitated, staring at the picture of two young boys, arms around each other, grinning.

"The taller boy on the left is my uncle Daniel, with his best friend, John, the old sheriff's nephew." She paused. "I never knew him, of course, but Mother, his sister, loved him so. It was just so terrible ..." Her voice trailed off.

"Now Maria," said Mrs. Kirk, "you know how upset you get when you talk about that." In a hushed voice to the boys, she said, "They drowned in a terrible accident."

Sean stammered, "Oh, gee ... I'm sorry."

"Oh, that's all right. Daniel is buried in Tolomato, you know," she said with pride. Then in a lower voice she said, "Took a lot of persuasion by the sheriff because the cemetery had already closed, but we have a lot of family there and it was important to his parents."

"Tolomato!" Matt exclaimed.

"What happened?" Sean quickly asked.

The boys noted Mrs. Kirk's disapproving look.

"I mean, well. I'm sorry, I guess you don't like to talk about it," Sean said.

Mrs. Masters, surprised by their curiosity, looked at the two youngsters. So refreshing, she thought, young folks showing an interest in history.

"Well, I'll tell you if you really want to know."

"Now, Maria, you—"

"No, it's all right," Mrs. Masters said. "I appreciate their interest."

She gazed at the picture.

"Well, it was a long time ago. My own mother was only nine." She paused. "She was crazy about Daniel. He and John were inseparable. John was staying with his uncle, the sheriff, and his little cousins at the time."

"He lived at the jail?" Matt cut in.

"Well, no, not permanently, but he stayed there often, especially in the summer. Mother said he enjoyed talking with the prisoners. He was usually a shy boy. It sounds as though Daniel, a strong, vigorous boy, was kind of like a big brother to John. I think he had family trouble—his father, you know." She shook her head. "I guess folks carried on about how it was probably all Daniel's fault because John

155

was too reserved and shy to think up such a thing. But that was all hogwash. They were only boys."

She reached up and touched the picture.

Matt and Sean were both thinking the same thing. This was either a weird coincidence or else ....

"Anyway," she said, continuing the story, "Daniel's father had bought him a small sailboat and was teaching Daniel how to sail." She smiled. "Mother said that boy idolized his father." She went on. "Well, late one night, the boys apparently decided to take the boat out, over on the bay." She shook her head slowly. "They just drowned."

She sat quietly, then caught herself. "They found pieces of the boat. Said it looked like something hit it. Then they found those poor little bodies, right over by the fort."

Mrs. Kirk sensed Mrs. Masters' sorrow. "Well, that's just all history. Such a shame, those young boys."

Neither Matt nor Sean could speak. A thousand questions filled their heads, but Mrs. Kirk's tone made it clear the story was over.

"Well, we bes' be going, Maria. You all right now, dear?" She patted the old lady's hand.

"Oh, of course. I sure appreciate you boys doing this little job for me. Can I pay you?" she asked.

"Oh, no ma'am. Happy to help," Matt responded, not wanting to leave the many questions he had, open.

Mrs. Kirk took charge. "Come on now, boys."

"Oh, there's my ladies," Mrs. Masters said as they stepped onto the porch. "Sean, please run and get my purse on that table by the door." She then called out to her friends.

"Mrs. Kirk, when did that accident happen?" Matt asked as Sean scurried away for the purse.

"Um, let's see. I think she said about 1900." Her brow furrowed as she recalled. "Yep. July 3, 1900." She took in a breath. "Oh my goodness, that's tomorrow. That poor dear." She turned to Matt. "You boys don't go asking her any more questions."

"Oh, no ma'am," Matt replied, startled that she was apparently reading his mind.

"Here you go, Grandma. Don't bring home any strangers," Sean said, handing over the purse.

"No, guess I won't do that." She chuckled. "You boys go in and get some cake and milk. It's OK to do that for breakfast sometimes. Not a lot, though." The old lady winked.

As the car pulled away, Jenny crossed the street.

"What are you guys doing? I didn't know Yankee boys got up this early."

"You want some cake? We need to catch you up." Matt looked at Sean. "You're not gonna believe this," he said to Jenny, with Sean nodding in agreement.

While they munched Mrs. Kirk's cake, the boys filled Jenny in on Matt and Hattie's jail encounter and Mrs. Masters' story.

"Holy cow!" she exclaimed. "You think—" She stopped abruptly. "We gotta go see Miss Hattie."

CHAPTER 21

Miss Hattie was rocking on the front porch when the cycle caravan arrived.

The youngsters approached the old woman with caution, unsure what her attitude might be to their impromptu visit.

"Can we talk to you, Miss Hattie?" Matt asked from a respectable distance.

"Not if it 'bout them spirits. I been thinking on it and I don't know how to help 'em," she said with finality. "Not yet, no how."

Matt said, "We know who the boys are."

"Which boys?"

"You know, in the jail and in the cemetery."

"So what if you did. What you gone do 'bout it?" She peered over the small-lens glasses perched halfway down her nose. "You best jus' leave it alone and stay away from that graveyard."

"Well, we don't know what to do, that's why we came to see you. Thought maybe you could help us figure out what's going on," Matt pleaded, ignoring the last part of Hattie's statement.

"I done told you I don't know neither." She sounded frustrated.

"Miss Hattie, those apparitions are just little boys. We were thinking if we shared all the information and talked about it, maybe we could figure something out," Jenny said, trying logic.

"Sugar, I feel as bad as you 'bout them children, but I done thought on it and ain't nothin' more to be said." She shook her head slowly. "Jus' don't see how any more gabbing could help."

"Well, can't we at least tell you how Matt and Sean found out who the boys might be and what happened to them?" Jenny asked, making a final plea.

Miss Hattie rocked without replying.

"Well, looks like you ain't gone leave anyway. Go ahead. Tell me," Hattie said, breaking the silence. "But then that is gone be it. I don't fancy listenin' to no more 'bout it. Feel bad enough 'bout them children." She made a slight tishing sound.

160

"Now go ahead on and say what you think you need to say."

Matt related the Masters' story, with Sean plugging in the gaps. When they finished, they stood silently, waiting for her response.

"She said that one boy lived in the jail and was best friends with that other one?"

"Yes ma'am."

She continued rocking. "Could be that jail boy ... say his name fo' me again." She looked at Matt.

"John. John was his name, and he stayed at the jail with his uncle, the sheriff," Matt quickly responded.

"Could be that John boy won't go up without his friend. Don't seem like anythin' holdin' him." She gave a short humph. "That ol' crazy Mary sho' ain't keepin' him from going."

She seemed to be reflecting, her brow furrowed with her struggle to recall. "She said sumthin' 'bout he was waitin' on his friend."

She lapsed back in silent thought for a moment, then continued, almost mumbling. "So looks like that John boy could go on up 'cause ain't nuttin' stopping him. Not ol' Mary. She ain't no evil spirit— knowed that right away."

She stopped talking again. The teens let out a breath and breathed again. They had been almost holding their breath to hear Hattie because she was talking so low, as if to herself.

"Anyhow, that other boy, one in that graveyard—might be that Daniel, might not. Don't matter 'cause he won't leave, and he in there with that ol' restless thing ... that thing mean, too, feedin' that poor boy nonsense."

She stopped rocking again and looked sternly at the boys. "You kids done somehow connected with them children and that evil thing in that graveyard knows it, so ol' Hattie tellin' you again, you best stay 'way from there."

She continued staring at the boys for effect. "Both them children scared. I jus' hate it." She rocked harder, as if to release her frustration on the rocker.

"You're talking about the poltergeist?" Jenny asked.

"I mean that evil spirit. Call 'em what you want, missy. He is evil and he's smart. Know'd what I was up to soon's I got to that ol' graveyard. Yep, he sho' 'nuff keepin' that boy there. Still, I 'spect he could leave if he truly wanted to. Mos' likely that ol' thing playin' with him." She removed her glasses and wiped her eyes. "Little sumthin' in ol' Hattie's eyes," she mumbled.

The teenagers realized that all these revelations were upsetting to the woman, and each in their own way was torn between concern for Hattie and the desire to resolve the strange situation.

"You done told me everything 'bout that John and Daniel. You didn't leave out nothing?" Hattie asked Matt.

"Well, yeah, like I told you, we—"

Sean cut in, deciding they may as well make sure everything was covered, though it didn't really seem relevant. "Oh, Mrs. Masters said they were best friends, always together, and when they drowned, folks blamed Daniel because they figured it was his idea to take the boat out. Oh, and he idolized his father."

But Hattie had stopped rocking. She looked like she was in a coma.

"Miss Hattie, what is it?" Jenny asked, fearing they had stressed the old lady too much.

Hattie stood and looked at the kids strangely, as if she were trying to make a decision.

Sean moved, about to speak, but Jenny gave him a subtle but dismissing sign. She watched Hattie carefully, not wanting the woman's chain of thought to be broken, certain she was sorting out some missing link in the puzzle.

"That boy Daniel, one in the graveyard, could be he's punishing himself 'cause he feels guilty he let everybody down. And that evil thing probably feedin' that 'cause he don't want him to go."

She stopped only long enough to catch her breath. "And could be that other boy, John, won't leave without his friend." She looked at Matt. "Remember what Mary said 'bout that?" she said.

Matt nodded.

"Where'd they find them boys?" she asked no one in particular.

"In the bay. By the fort," Sean answered.

"And that ol' Mary said that boy goes to the fort sometime for something or other." She was thinking out loud more than actually speaking to the teens. "And she said he's probably goin' soon. What date did them children drown?"

"July third," Matt said.

"Oh my soul," Hattie muttered.

"You think ..." Jenny realized what Hattie was thinking.

Hattie spoke before Jenny could complete her thought.

"That boy is goin' to that ol' fort to look for his friend. They left from there and got stuck in between." She shook her head. "That's got to be it, and he sure gonna go tomorrow, July third," she added.

They stared at each other, dumbfounded.

"Come up here. All of you. Come on up here." Hattie motioned to the youngsters to step onto the porch.

"Now, you children listen to me. You want to help them boys?" she asked.

"Yes ma'am," they all responded.

She looked from one to the other.

"You got to get that Daniel boy out of that cemetery tomorrow night 'cause his friend is gone be at the bay by that fort waitin' on him. I know it."

"But how? You said he won't leave. He feels too guilty," Jenny asked.

"Love," the old lady said simply.

Jenny repeated, "Love."

"You know about love, missy?"

"Well, I, I guess …." Jenny glanced at Matt.

Hattie saw the subtle look and smiled. "You gotta get that woman, his relative, to go there with you and talk to him. Late, so no one else is around and he'll more likely to show himself," Hattie explained.

"Mrs. Masters?" Matt said.

"Yes, Mrs. Masters. He might connect with her."

"Mrs. Masters," Matt said again, thinking of the old lady and how proper she was. "She'll never do it." He shook his head. "Go to the Tolomato Cemetery late at night to talk to a ghost."

He looked at Sean and Jenny, searching for a sign that he was wrong, but their looks held the same conclusion.

Matt said, "She won't do it, Hattie. Besides, what about that evil spirit?"

"That boy can leave if he wants to bad enough. She got to convince him nobody blames him and they love him." She looked at Jenny. "You understand, missy? You know what ol' Hattie sayin'?"

Jenny held Hattie's soft gaze. "We'll get her to go. Will you come?" Jenny said with determination as the boys looked at each other.

"Sure, I'm coming. You need some help with that evil spirit." Her eyes twinkled. "Samuel gone take me to that cemetery at eleven o'clock tomorrow night. If you ain't there with that woman, I'm gone go on home." She put her hand on Jenny's arm. "But I 'speck you gone get her on down there."

She stood up and turned toward the door. She opened the screen door and looked back over her shoulder. "Go on now, and talk about what you got to do. It'll come to you."

As they reached their cycles Matt said, "We need to go back to Mrs. Masters' house."

"Yeah. We need to tell her." Sean nodded his head in agreement.

"So you two masterminds are just gonna waltz in and convince an old lady, a science teacher no less, to go to a cemetery late at night." She looked at the boys in disbelief, hands on her hips.

Matt stopped fumbling with his helmet. "I see your point," he said, suddenly feeling a little foolish.

"Yeah," Sean agreed. "Well, what then?"

They both looked to Jenny for direction.

"We need Mrs. Kirk to help us," Jenny stated without hesitation.

"Grandma!" Sean exclaimed.

"Yes, dummy, Grandma. She and Mrs. Masters have known each other practically their entire lives."

Sean mumbled, "I don't know ..."

"Jenny's right, Sean. We need Mrs. Kirk. I say we go see her right now," Matt said.

"Anyway, she's gone to Flagler, remember? Won't be back until after we're at work." Sean sounded relieved.

"Oh, that's right," Jenny said. "OK. We'll talk to her first thing in the morning, when she's not so tired. Then we can go next door and see Mrs. Masters."

"Yeah. That's good. Also give us time to think through everything," Matt agreed.

Sean remained quiet, deep in thought.

"Come on, man. What else can we do?" Matt pleaded.

"We really don't have any other reasonable choices, Sean," Jenny, ever the psychologist, added.

"OK," Sean said reluctantly. "But let me talk to her alone first." He added, "If she'll do it, I'll call you guys over."

"What if she won't do it?" Matt asked, looking at Jenny.

"Not an option. She's our only hope. I don't think we could get Mrs. Masters to do it by ourselves." She spoke directly to Sean. "You have to convince your grandmother to help, Yankee boy. You sure you don't want us to come?"

"No. I'll do it. First thing tomorrow morning."

CHAPTER 22

The gentle sounds of small waves were broken by frantic splashing. Splintered boards and slivers of wood bumped the young bodies as they struggled to stay afloat.

A voice cried out as the boy floundered in the dark water. The pale light of the moon reflected off his frightened face. He paddled his small hands frantically, searching the water around him.

He heard a moan and cried out, but water filled his mouth, gagging him. Even so, he moved toward the outstretched arm with all the strength his weakening body could muster.

The two small hands touched, and the boys disappeared into the depths of the unforgiving darkness.

Matt sat up in bed, gasping for breath. He looked around and his breathing slowed when he became aware of the familiar surroundings of his bedroom bathed by the light of a full moon.

He could not stop thinking of the impending meeting with Mrs. Masters. They needed her help, but how could she possibly believe their story? He wasn't sure he would believe it had he not experienced the events.

He glanced at the eerie red glow of the clock. Three fifteen. With a sigh of resignation, he lay his head on the pillow and pulled the covers up to soothe the sudden shiver he felt. There would be no sleep this night.

CHAPTER 23

July 3, A.M.

When the bedroom door opened and his mom stuck her head in, Matt was fully dressed.

"Sean called, honey. He said he needed you to come over." She studied her son's tired face. "What are you guys up to?"

But Matt was already past her, headed to the front door.

"Matt." Jenny scurried down her front porch where she had been perched for some time. "What did Sean say?"

"Didn't talk to him yet," he replied, heading across the street where Sean waited on his steps.

"Did you tell her? What did she say?" Matt asked abruptly.

"I told her. She wants to see all of us."

"Will she help?" Jenny asked.

"I don't know. Maybe," he said slowly. "Let's go in."

"Come in, kids. Sit down," Mrs. Kirk said.

They sat down without speaking.

The old woman looked from one to the other, causing the boys to shift uncomfortably.

"What you children are asking me to do cannot be taken lightly," she stated. "Maria— Mrs. Masters—is getting on up there in years, and you know she has that heart problem." She stopped speaking and sat for a moment, gathering her thoughts.

"Now, Sean has assured me that you kids ain't just having some fun with this incredible story, and that he really saw spirits. I believe him." She looked at Jenny. "Now, honey, I want you to tell me exactly what you saw, and then," she shifted her eyes to Matt, "I want you to do the same thing."

Jenny told her version in a cool, methodical manner, as if delivering a classroom lecture; her planned move was to sound more adult and formal as opposed to a babbling kid.

Matt watched with envy as she finished, relieved Jenny had gone first but also aware that hers would be a hard act to follow.

He cleared his suddenly dry throat and recounted his experiences.

When he finished talking, the ticking grandfather clock filled the otherwise quiet room with its steady rhythm.

"I don't know," the old lady finally mumbled. "It's just so incredible." She fell silent again, then added, with a caring look, "It isn't that I don't believe you. I do believe you all saw something ..." She trailed off, obviously wrestling with her own doubts about the request, and concern for her friend next door.

"I dreamed about 'em last night," Matt said softly.

"What was that, son?" Mrs. Kirk said quietly to Matt.

"Last night. I dreamed about the boys, in the water." His eyes were moist.

Jenny touched his arm.

"Oh, honey," Mrs. Kirk murmured.

With a long sigh, she reached for the phone next to her chair, then pulled her arm back. "I'm gonna go with you, but if Maria starts getting upset, I want you three to leave us. You understand?"

"Yes ma'am," they all responded.

Mrs. Kirk took a deep breath and picked up the phone.

CHAPTER 24

The glad-to-see-you's were exchanged, and Mrs. Masters, looking puzzled about the arrival of this unlikely group of visitors, opened the door wider in proper fashion and invited them in.

"I'm sorry, I don't have anything ready to offer you," she said. "But I could make some sweet tea."

Mrs. Kirk was shaking her head. "Oh, no," she said. "We came by to see you for a moment, and I'm so sorry for this inconvenience."

"Oh, not at all, dear. It's a lovely surprise. I don't get many visitors, you know."

"Maria," Mrs. Kirk began, in a hesitant manner, "do you remember several years ago when I told you that little story about the couple I had seen in my garden?"

"Why, yes. Yes I do," Maria responded, shocked because her friend had sworn her to secrecy at the time she told her the story.

Sean gave his grandmother a surprised glance.

"Well, these children wanted to tell you something that's, well, kind of like that."

Maria looked confused.

"It involves Daniel," Mrs. Kirk added softly.

"Daniel?" Mrs. Masters glanced at the picture hanging on her wall. "I-I don't understand."

"I know how it must sound, but I want you to know that I would never be surprising you like this if I did not think it was important. Now, it is an, uh, well, I guess one could say, an unusual story. But I am convinced these young folks are telling the truth."

"What kind of story? Karen, what on earth is going on?"

"Well, if you don't mind, I'm just gonna let Jenny here tell the story," Mrs. Kirk said, deciding at the last second that Jenny would be the best choice.

Both boys looked relieved. Jenny sat composed, her mind already laying out the presentation.

After gauging Maria's reaction carefully, Mrs. Kirk continued. "Now, I will understand perfectly should you want Jenny to stop." Receiving no response, she turned to Jenny. "Go ahead, Jenny."

Jenny, taking the cue, presented the story, talking in a calm, organized manner, while glancing occasionally at Mrs. Kirk for reassurance.

She finished recounting the experience, leaving out the cemetery trip plan, noted with an approving nod from Mrs. Kirk.

"Well, my goodness, I-I ...." Maria was bewildered.

"Maria, I know how this must sound, your background and all," Mrs. Kirk said, referring to her friend's career in science. "But these children are all good kids, and they really believe what they saw."

"Well, yes, I can see that," Maria responded, looking at the youngsters. "But I, well, I don't understand, why are you telling me this?" She looked at Mrs. Kirk. "Karen, I don't know why you would want to remind me of that terrible tragedy. And now, to suggest that those poor boys have not gone on." She paused. "I don't know why you would do that."

"I know, I know, Maria. And I really would have no part of this, but these children think you can help Daniel. Both of those boys, John too." Mrs. Kirk feared they may have gone too far.

"Help them. How? I don't understand."

Mrs. Kirk did not answer, trying to decide whether or not to continue.

Jenny took her opportunity. "Mrs. Masters, we think there's a chance we can free those boys, their spirits. But we need your help."

Mrs. Masters sat silently, overwhelmed, but appeared surprisingly calm.

Jenny looked at Mrs. Kirk, who was studying her friend.

"Go ahead, Jenny. Tell her about Miss Hattie."

Jenny described their meetings with Miss Hattie and explained her plan about the cemetery visit.

She finished, thought for a moment, then reiterated that Mrs. Masters was the key to convincing Daniel that he should not punish himself, that his parents loved him and, more, wanted to be with him, and that his friend, John, was waiting for him.

"Oh my goodness, my goodness, I, I ...." Mrs. Masters began fanning her flushed face with her hand.

"Maria, I'm so sorry. I know this is upsetting and impossible to believe. I know you, of all people, find it hard to believe such things, but I ...." Her voice trailed off.

Several moments passed. The scene was a replay of Mrs. Kirk's house moments earlier, with the sound of a grandfather clock and two other wall clocks dominating the room.

A strange-looking carved figure popped out of the front of one wall clock as the timepiece started counting off, causing the teens to jump. Mrs. Kirk sat perfectly still, watching her close friend, praying she had not forever altered their close relationship.

Without speaking, Mrs. Masters rose and walked to the picture of Daniel and John. She reached out and touched it gently, then slowly straightened it, just so.

Her back still to the group, she began to speak in a soft voice. "Mother was always straightening this picture. I really believe it was merely an excuse to touch it. She loved her brother Daniel so." She paused and touched the picture again. "The last weeks of Mother's life, she asked us to set her bed up in here so she could be around all the precious things that were her family." She waved a hand toward the heirlooms and memorabilia scattered around the room. "We got her a little bell, that little bell." She pointed to a small silver bell adjacent to the picture, on a shelf made for that purpose. "When she needed something, she would ring the bell. Each time the bell rang, I would come and see to her needs, and always she would ask me to straighten the picture." She smiled. "It was almost never crooked, but it made her feel good." She paused again.

"Mother died, and for days afterwards I would, on occasion, hear the bell. At first I responded, I'm sure, out of habit, and of course nothing was there. I didn't know what to make of it. I began ignoring the bell when it rang, believing, in my grief I was simply imagining things. It kept on, but actually started ringing louder; so loud that I ran to the room on one occasion, convinced someone had to be there ringing the bell.

"There was no one. It was very distressing. I turned to leave the room but noticed the picture was slightly askew, so I straightened it. When I did so, I clearly heard a sigh ... a contented sigh." She turned and faced the group. "After that, I never heard the bell again."

The old lady dabbed at her moist eyes and looked at her dear friend. "Karen, when you told me about that couple you saw, I did believe you. You could never lie, but sometimes we can be too logical, too scientific. There's so much that's difficult to understand so we take the easy way out—we don't believe it." She smiled again. "I do believe, and I believe you children. If there is even the remotest chance we can help those boys, of course I'll go."

"You will?" Sean exclaimed.

Mrs. Kirk stood and went to her friend, clasping her hands tightly.

Jenny kissed Matt lightly on the cheek, a tear from her cheek touching his face. Their emotions were drained.

"Well, you all go see that Miss Hattie and get things organized. Maria and I are gonna sit a spell," Mrs. Kirk told the youngsters, looking to Maria for approval.

"Yes. Stay, Karen. Let's talk."

"Oh, kids," Mrs. Masters said as the youngsters turned to go. "Supposed to be one of them summer storms tonight, so everybody bring a hat and umbrella."

"Yes ma'am," the threesome yelled back as they bolted out the door.

CHAPTER 25

As the unlikely group caravanned to the cemetery and parked in the Oldest Drugstore parking lot, the promised storm was taking shape.

The heat and oppression of the still air resulting from the building storm increased as the late evening wore on.

The night, appropriately, was absolutely dark. Not even a twinkle of star could penetrate the cloud that consumed the sky.

A dog foraging around the drugstore Dumpster next to the cemetery fence glanced curiously at the group, then continued his meal.

Though they knew the streets would be empty at this late hour, and a storm warning had been issued, the side gate off the main thoroughfare was chosen for their entry point to ensure privacy.

Hot air blew over them as they neared the gate, though there was no wind whatever. Immediately after, thunder crackled just above the cemetery and a flash of lightning gave no reassurance to their pounding hearts.

Hattie fondled the simple brass lock securing the gate chain. She produced a small, sharp object and deftly played with the mechanism until it sprang open.

They started in and a loud moan ensued.

Hattie stopped and removed the cap from a small tin she had retrieved from her pocket. She poked a gnarled finger inside and smeared salve on her upper lip, under her nose.

"Pass this 'round. Everybody put some on," she instructed the group.

She started in again and was pelted with a mass of debris seemingly blown at her. She fell to the ground, mumbling.

Samuel was quickly by her side, grabbing for her arms.

"Git on back now. Caught me 'fore I was ready," she told Samuel as she regained her feet and took a small leather pouch from her neck.

She threw powder from the pouch toward the now swirling path of leaves and debris in front of them. To the amazement of the on-lookers, the substance penetrated the swirling mass and went into the cemetery.

"How you like that, spirit?" she called out.

Her challenge was answered as a form materialized, its shape outlined by the same dancing electric sparks she had seen before.

The dog had his hackles up, his lips curled back from his teeth and his growl grew louder. Suddenly his courage deserted him and with a frightened yelp, he scuttled away, tail tucked between his sprinting legs.

The powder continued to flow.

Hattie called out, "You, boy, Daniel, come on out here. This ol' spirit can't hurt you."

A glow appeared to the right rear.

"Tha's right, come on now. This evil thing jus' thinks he holding you but he's not."

The dancing light flashes grew larger and a shape resembling a human form could be seen. The glow that was Daniel dimmed.

"Woman, you, Maria, come on here. Talk to that boy," she directed Mrs. Masters.

"Daniel, Daniel, it's me. Maria. I'm your niece," she said in a quivering voice. "I'm Margareta's daughter." Remembering Daniel had never met her, she had clarity enough to add, "Your sister, Margareta."

The bluish-white light moved across the cemetery toward them, growing brighter, taking shape.

A loud, indescribable cry came from the mass of swirling, arcing sparks. A large, deep hollowness could be seen where eyes should have been.

Trees in the cemetery were rattling and whipping around furiously, though outside the fence it was still the calm before the storm.

The approaching glow of Daniel dimmed again.

Hattie commanded, "Quick, woman, talk. His parents. Talk."

"Daniel, Margareta loved you so. You're all she ever talked about. The fun you had and how much your parents loved you. We all love you," Mrs. Masters, now in somewhat more control, recalled her mother's words. "Daniel, they knew it wasn't your fault. They forgave you. They love you and want you with them."

The shape, clearly a young boy, grew brighter and approached again.

A foul smell became evident as the evil grew even larger and lunged at Daniel. He dimmed slightly and retreated.

"Daniel, John is waiting for you. Over by the fort. He's stuck because he won't leave without you. Go to him, don't disappoint him." The science teacher reasoning with a student took over in Mrs. Masters.

Hattie started yelling wildly at the sparking, thrashing form. She threw more powder at the now snarling, hollow, growing mass of evil moving toward Daniel's glow.

But this time Daniel seemed to grow brighter and darted away from the mass lunging at him.

"That's it, boy," Hattie yelled out, "fight that evil thing!"

Mrs. Masters called out, "Daniel, go to John. He's there now, waiting. They're all waiting, Daniel. Go to them now."

The brightly glowing Daniel seemed to be pulling up against some force, as if he could not free himself.

Overhead, the thunder of the storm cracked and roared. The rustle of more movement in the cemetery seemed to surround them. The evil spirit sent limbs and rocks flying in all directions while the other movement became more active.

"They're helping him. The others. Keep talkin'," Hattie directed Mrs. Masters.

"Daniel, you were the strongest. John needs you. Go to him. He's your best friend."

The surrounding movement intensified and the glow that was the young boy grew so bright, Hattie held a hand up to shield her eyes.

In an almost violent motion, Daniel's form surged upward as if a chain had snapped. It moved, almost drifting, a wavy, glowing form, toward the bay.

The crackling, growling, dark mass of sparks shot upward in pursuit.

"Come on!" Matt yelled to Sean, and turned to run but stopped, looking back at the old women and Samuel.

"Go on, go on. I got these ladies," Samuel urged them.

CHAPTER 26

The youngsters dashed around the drugstore and started sprinting up Orange Street for the bay, about two hundred yards ahead.

As they passed the Old City Gate on St. George Street, directly across from the fort, they could see the glow off to their right in the dark sky that had to be Daniel. The other thing was trailing him.

They looked back toward the fort. Hattie was right.

Directly over the old structure another glow, dimmer, could be seen.

"Hey, you boys!" An elderly policeman had been watching them and was clearly suspicious of their behavior. He grabbed Matt's arm.

"Gene. Gene. Let 'em go."

"Mrs. Kirk?" he responded when he recognized the woman.

"Please let 'em go, Gene. I'll explain later."

He released Matt's arm.

By now, the two young spirits were glowing brightly.

A lone car screeched to a halt.

"What the he—" A tourist, digital camera in hand, jumped out, followed by another man.

"Frank, what is that?" the passenger asked.

The man, busy snapping pictures, did not answer.

The storm had arrived. Thunder was rolling constantly and the lightning strikes surrounded them.

The two glowing forms had stopped, as if only now realizing each other's presence. They grew brighter and moved toward each other.

A loud bellow, heard above the thunder, came from the trailing mass approaching the boys' spirits. It appeared to gain speed when suddenly a lightning bolt hit the jumping sparks with a resounding crack. The form dimmed, even as the two boys brightened the dark sky. A slender, waving thread from each shape extended out, touched and merged as one bright glow ... and disappeared.

"Holy cow!" The tourist was trying to review his digital pictures, his passenger peering over his shoulder.

"There's nothing here." He hit the button furiously. "I didn't get nuttin'," he moaned.

"Weren't nuttin', no how," Samuel said to the man. "Jus' one of them ol' Ancient City storms." He winked at Hattie.

The rain started, running the tourists to their car.

"Well, Karen, I don't know what's goin' on here, but looks under control now. Any idea about what we just saw?" the cop said.

"Why, Gene, you know the Old Town got ghosts everywhere."

He laughed. "OK. If you folks are all right, I think I'll get on outta this rain."

"We're fine, Gene. We'll do the same. Have a good night," the old lady responded.

They all had umbrellas, but none were open.

Mrs. Masters looked toward the sky and let the rain wash over her face. "Feels good, don't it, Karen?"

Mrs. Kirk took her hand. "Yes, Maria, it truly does feel good."

"Well, I don't know 'bout you all, but I'm 'bout ready to be outta this rain and definitely that lightning," Samuel said, reminding everyone of the situation.

"Well, half the night's gone. Everybody go to my house. I believe I might have some leftover cake," Mrs. Kirk announced.

"Gee, I'm so surprised," Sean said, and laughed as they all turned to go.

Jenny reached out to hold Matt's hand. "So, you gonna take me to all those great July Fourth events tomorrow or what?"

"Me. I, ah, well, yeah. You bet."

Jenny opened her umbrella and handed it to Matt. "Here, you hold the shelter." She took her hand from the handle and looped it through his arm, pressing close. "I think it'll cover both of us if we stay close."

It did. But Matt didn't notice the rain.

About the Author

Randy Cribbs, shown here with Murphy, is a native of Florida. A retired Army officer, he is the recipient of **two 2007 FPA President's Best Book Awards; a 2006 FWA Royal Palm Literary Best Book Award and was selected as a 2005 Much Ado About Books featured author.** He holds degrees from the University of Florida, Pacific Lutheran University, Jacksonville State University and is a graduate of the FBI National Academy and the Armed Forces Staff College. He is the author of seven books: *Were You There? Vietnam Notes; Tales from the Oldest City; One Summer in the Old Town; Illumination Rounds; The Vessel ... tinaja: An Ancient City Mystery; Ancient City Treasures and Ghosts: Another Summer in the Old Town.* He currently resides in St. Augustine, Florida.

www.somestillserve.com

ONE SUMMER IN THE OLD TOWN

Randy draws the reader into a summer adventure set in St. Augustine and on the banks of the St. Johns River. A well-researched, historical overview of the nation's oldest city is woven into the fast paced story through a host of colorful characters. A great story and an interesting, fun way to learn about the history, landmarks, and mystique of the Old Town; it includes original drawings by artist, Manilla Clough.

Used by schools and book clubs throughout the region, this book is enjoyed by all ages.

TALES FROM THE OLDEST CITY

The author's affection for the nation's oldest city and old Florida is evident in this colorful collection of short stories. From the mystery of 'So Little Time', and adventure of 'Mike's Birds' to the heartwarming 'Riverman', humor of 'Peanuts' and romance of 'Tattoo', readers are presented with a broad variety of tales guaranteed to tickle the imagination. Randy's ability to blend fact and fiction into entertaining stories makes this picturesque tour through the Old Town a special way to visit and revisit the unique places, history, and colorful characters of St. Augustine, the St. Johns River , and surrounding area.

THE VESSEL ...TINAJA

When the body of archaeologist William Stewart is found floating in the bay, a curious reporter finds himself caught up in a web of hideous secrets, deceit, and murder woven by the lure of the tinaja and its terrifying power.

At first his empirical mind refuses to believe the old Indian story. As he is drawn deeper into Stewart's past and his own deadly lover's triangle, each ghastly revelation points to an unimaginable power and moves him dangerously close to the line that separates right from wrong, fact from myth; and now, that power may be within his grasp.

"Was Ponce De Leon pursuing the wrong object for everlasting youth?"

Printed in the United States
127749LV00001B/1/P

9 780972 579674